Make Me Love You

Elizabeth Bright

This book is a work of fiction. Names, characters, places, and incidents are products of the writer's imagination or are used fictitiously and are not to be construed as real. Any resemblance to actual events, locales, or persons, living or dead, is entirely coincidental.

Make Me Love You

Copyright © 2021 by Elizabeth Bright. All rights reserved.

Cover Design by Wildheart Graphics

Editing by Mackenzie Walton

No part of this work may be used, reproduced, or transmitted in any form or by any means without prior permission in writing from the author, except in the case of brief quotations utilized in critical articles or reviews.

Digital ISBN: 978-1-7370702-0-7

Paperback ISBN: 978-1-7370702-1-4

Contents

1. Chapter 1 — 1
2. Chapter 2 — 15
3. Chapter 3 — 23
4. Chapter 4 — 35
5. Chapter 5 — 45
6. Chapter 6 — 55
7. Chapter 7 — 65
8. Chapter 8 — 81
9. Chapter 9 — 97
10. Chapter 10 — 111
11. Chapter 11 — 121
12. Chapter 12 — 129

13. Chapter 13   137

14. Chapter 14   147

15. Chapter 15   157

16. Chapter 16   161

17. Chapter 17   177

18. Chapter 18   187

19. Chapter 19   193

20. Chapter 20   207

21. Chapter 21   215

22. Chapter 22   225

23. Chapter 23   233

24. Chapter 24   243

25. Chapter 25   253

26. Chapter 26   263

27. Chapter 27   273

28. Chapter 28   281

29. Chapter 29   291

30. Chapter 30   301

31. Chapter 31   313

32. Chapter 32   321

33.	Chapter 33	329
34.	Chapter 34	341
35.	Chapter 35	345
Acknowledgements		353
About the Author		355
Also By Elizabeth Bright		357

Chapter 1

Emma

It said something that the town of Hart's Ridge, North Carolina, was named for the mountain peaks that encircled it like a halo rather than for the valley in which it was actually located. Maybe it said that the people of Hart's Ridge were optimists, that they were always looking up.

Then again, maybe they were always looking up because they knew the minute they turned their backs, the volatile mountain weather would bite them in the butt.

I leaned out the window of my Airstream-turned-food-truck, my gaze tracking the straight line down Main Street to where Hart Mountain loomed behind City Hall like a sentry. There wasn't a cloud in the sky, except a benign puffy white type here and there. I narrowed my eyes.

Yep. Definitely a bite-you-in-the-butt kind of day.

"Ain't no point in staring out that window, Emma." Cesar Martinez, my business partner and surrogate grandfather, didn't bother to look up from his book to verify the truth of his statement. "Nobody's coming."

I sighed. Only a month ago, we would have sold a couple hundred cups of coffee and twice that in burritos. My Airstream was the last stop on Main Street before the road turned to ten miles of nothingness that stretched all the way to the chicken processing plant. The processing plant employed nearly a thousand workers, which meant every morning a hefty portion of those workers swung by on the way into work to pick up coffee and a breakfast burrito, and maybe a second burrito to save for lunch.

The processing plant that had, exactly one month ago, given formal notice to its thousand employees that it was consolidating its operations in Delaware. The North Carolina operations were shutting down. The law required sixty days' notice, but now thirty days in, the plant was already nearly deserted.

Workers who commuted in from other towns had no reason to come to Hart's Ridge now—they weren't going

MAKE ME LOVE YOU 3

to make that drive just for Cesar's burritos, even if they were the best burritos east of the Mississippi and north of Mexico. Some workers had probably left for Delaware. A good number lived in Hart's Ridge, but who knew if they would stay? In a town of less than four thousand, there weren't many jobs to go around.

All of which meant we'd had a grand total of six customers that morning.

Six. That wasn't enough to cover my *own* wages, much less Cesar's. Cesar was sixty-nine and needed the job. And if I couldn't cover myself and Cesar, then I definitely couldn't cover my dad. He'd be home in four months—four *months,* good Lord—and who was going to hire him if not me? The good folks of Hart's Ridge were not exactly lining up to hire themselves a convicted felon.

And what about—

No. I halted the doom train in its tracks before it could run away with my sanity, breathing in through my nose and out through my mouth. It wouldn't do me any good to go down that path. I needed solutions, not nausea.

"What are we going to do?" I asked, as much of the universe as of Cesar.

Cesar leaned against the oak cabinet that stretched from floor to roof, folded his arms over his chest, and crossed one long leg over the other. "I figure you will come up with something."

"Why in the heck would you figure that?" I demanded.

"Because that's what you do. You make it work. Eight years ago, your life was a mess. Mom dead, dad in jail, no money. A house that needed upkeep and this trailer that had seen better days. You didn't know how to cook, didn't know how to get this thing running. Look at you now."

I blinked. That was a pretty generous assessment of my life and glossed over quite a bit of failure. College, for example. I hadn't been able to keep up with classes and a job waitressing at Dreamer's Cafe, which I'd needed to pay the mortgage and basic necessities like food and soap. I'd flunked my classes before dropping out altogether—to the surprise of absolutely no one.

As for fixing up the Airstream, yeah, I had done that, with Cesar's help and a lot of internet tutorials. It was honestly amazing what you could learn on the internet these days.

"You made it work. Though," he amended, "you still can't cook."

"I can cook," I protested.

"You can follow instructions. There's a difference."

Considering that my cooking consisted of tortillas, scrambled eggs, sauteed vegetables, and heating beans that

Cesar had worked some magic on the night prior, I had to admit he had a point. Cesar was responsible for everything that tasted good.

When I had first come up with this hare-brained idea, born of sheer desperation, I'd provided the Airstream—a relic from my family's happier life before Mom's cancer diagnosis—and he'd provided the skills. We made a good team.

"Well, I haven't come up with anything," I grumped. "What am I supposed to do, chain myself to the plant until they agree to stay?"

Cesar shrugged, completely unconcerned, as though both our livelihoods weren't at stake. "You'll think of something."

I slapped a dishrag against the counter and then did it again twice more, for good measure. I felt helpless, and I *hated* feeling helpless. I couldn't even clean anything—my go-to for stress relief—because without customers, the Airstream was already spotless.

"So, what, if I don't come up with something, the town is just going to fall down around our ears? The processing plant was the biggest employer in Hart's Ridge. Small towns die when they lose income like that."

"Yeah, yeah, go tell the mayor," Cesar said drily.

The mayor.

Someone who could actually *do* something. Supposedly. And even if he couldn't, it would make me feel better to yell at someone.

"I *will* tell the mayor. See if I won't." I untied my apron and hung it on its hook. Underneath I wore a plain white T-shirt, jeans, and scuffed sneakers that had more than one hole. Mom would have told me to wear a nice dress if I was going to yell at someone important, but Mom wasn't here to stop me. Cesar just shook his head. He was used to me by now. "You good here without me?"

Cesar made a big deal about looking left and looking right. "But what about all the customers?"

"Shut up," I growled, already halfway out the door.

"You walking?"

"Yeah." It was only a couple blocks. Not worth taking my truck.

"Take an umbrella. Storm's coming."

I glanced up at the nearly blue sky. The lone cloud had increased to four. But I wasn't fooled by that. The air had that thick, humid feel that promised a summer dumping, and the clouds might be puffy like cotton balls on top, but underneath they were flat and quickly darkening. "Not until this afternoon."

The May heat was intense, but that didn't stop me from walking as fast as I could. It felt good to stomp on the sidewalk, to move my muscles. Frustration made my stride long and purposeful, covering ground at a rapid pace. I was nearly there when I caught sight of a police car moseying by.

No.

Instantly I hunched my shoulders and ducked behind a lamp post, trying to make myself as invisible as possible. Not that I was afraid of being arrested—I'd never had so much as a parking ticket, thank you very much—I just didn't want to see *him*.

Eli Carter. My one-time best friend until he'd arrested my dad eight years ago for cooking meth. Which, okay, I understood that cooking meth wasn't a great way to spend time and also it's highly illegal. But he was my best friend. The one person I thought I could turn to.

The black paint on the lamp post was chipped in several places. I peeled anxiously at it with my thumbnail, holding my breath until I saw the number on the car: 699, not 701. It wasn't him. I glanced around, hoping no one saw me being weird with the lamp post, and then continued to City Hall.

I was walking much slower now, thrown off by the not-Eli sighting. In truth, I shouldn't be so worried. I hadn't really seen him in eight years, not since that night I'd told him I never wanted to see him again. It shouldn't have been possible to avoid a person for eight years in a small town that had two gas stations, one grocery store, and not much in the way of entertainment. I should have run into him constantly. But I didn't.

Apparently, he had taken me at my word. Oh, I'd seen glimpses of him here and there, at a party or around town, but he was always gone so quickly I was never completely sure it was him or wishful thinking.

No, not wishful thinking. The opposite of wishful thinking, whatever that was. Fearful thinking?

I was so lost in my thoughts that I found myself staring at the mayor's door without any memory of having arrived. I shook my head to clear my mind and then rapped sharply on the oak door.

"Come in!" Mayor Whittaker bellowed. He glanced up as I entered. "Ah, Emma. What can I do for you? Nothing to do with angles and planes, I hope."

I bit my lip, abashed. Before retiring five years ago, Mayor Whittaker had been the tenth-grade geometry teacher at John Hart High School. Geometry wasn't my best subject—although, to be fair, I didn't have a best subject. I was a B-average student—a source of endless disappointment and frustration to my education-minded parents—with a couple A's and C's sprinkled in. Geometry had been a C, and I had worked my butt off for it.

But I could tell from the twinkle in his eyes that Mayor Whittaker didn't realize his joke stung, so I shrugged it off. I wasn't here for geometry, anyway.

"You can tell me how I'm to keep my business open when the chicken plant closes, that's what you can do for me," I snapped.

Ignoring the fact that I hadn't been invited to take a seat, I yanked back a chair and plopped down on the cracked vinyl cushion, a shade of putrid pea green that suggested it was a relic of the 1960s. Which it probably was.

"People came from all over western North Carolina to work in the factory, and they stopped by my place every morning for breakfast on their way in," I told him. "No one's coming in anymore. They're staying in their own towns, or they're moving to Delaware. What are you going to do about that?"

Mr. Whittaker leaned forward, resting his elbows on his desk, and steepled his fingers. He peered at me over the rim of his glasses. "Sounds like a job for the mayor."

I loved Mr. Whittaker. He looked like Santa Claus. So much so, in fact, that he dressed up every year and read "'Twas the Night Before Christmas" to kids at the library. But right then, I wanted to strangle him, and I didn't care if that got me coal in my stocking.

"Yes," I said, struggling for patience. "That's why I'm here. You're the mayor."

"Hm." He pondered that. "How old are you now, Emma?"

"Twenty-eight. What's that got to do with anything?"

"A person must be twenty-five or older. It's one of the two qualifications for mayor. The other one being that a person can't otherwise be employed by the town. Which you aren't." He leaned back and grinned like a fox in a hen house. "Have at it."

A bad feeling settled in the pit of my stomach. "Have at what?"

"Have at being mayor."

"No, thank you." I laughed. It was a joke. It *had* to be a joke. But Mr. Whittaker didn't laugh. He stared at me patiently.

I stopped laughing.

"But *you're* the mayor."

"Turned in my resignation to City Council last Monday. My final duty is to find someone to act as mayor until a special election can be held."

"You can't be serious."

He sighed. "I'm tired, Emma. *Sick* and tired, if you want to know the truth. Doctor O'Hare says if I don't get my blood pressure under control I'm not long for this world.

When I first ran for mayor five years ago—unopposed, you remember—I was newly retired. I thought this would give me something to do and be a nice way to give back to the community I love so much. I still love it, but I can't do it anymore. My wife and I are heading out to California, where Cecily moved with her husband. We want to see our grandkids every day."

My heart sank into my beat-up Converse sneakers. The Whittakers were a Hart's Ridge institution—and Mrs. Whittaker was the deputy mayor. That was two positions to fill.

"It's time for us to go, Emma. We need to find someone to step up."

"And I'm the best you've got." I slumped in my chair.

"Not exactly." He frowned. "You weren't my first choice. Everyone else said no."

Well, wasn't that a kick in the teeth. I wasn't the best hope. I was the last resort.

"Look, it's two months. That's all. You don't even have to do very much. Keep your door open from eight to ten every morning for residents to bend your ear, sign some things now and again, and that's it. Heck, you don't even get a salary."

My eyes bugged out. "What? You mean I have to work for free?"

"Why do you think I'm having such a dickens of a time finding a replacement? Everyone is busy with their own thing, things that actually make money." He laughed. "Now, don't you worry, I've already found someone to act as deputy mayor and help you out a bit."

"I didn't say yes."

His shoulders drooped. "I'm sick," he reminded me.

I glared, even while my insides softened. A pox on my kind heart. It was nothing but trouble. "That's cruel, Mr. Whittaker. You're not playing fair."

"Is that a yes?"

"Yes." I regretted my answer the instant it left my lips. But what else could I do? I couldn't say no, not to Mr. Whittaker.

"Wonderful." He beamed. "Don't look so glum, Emma. It's only two months, to give City Council enough time to hold a special election for my replacement. We're halfway through May. You'll have to sign off on some Fourth of July celebrations and permits, but budget talks don't start until August. You'll be off the hook and some other sucker—" He caught himself and cleared his throat. "I mean, citizen. Some other *citizen* will take the helm."

I eyed him suspiciously. "You said you ran unopposed. I don't recall you ever having an opponent, in fact."

"Afraid no one else will step up to the plate? Don't you worry about that, my girl." He leaned forward and patted my hand encouragingly. "Someone always wants power, even in a small town like Hart's Ridge."

I opened my mouth to respond, but a knock on the door silenced me.

"Ah, good. That will be the acting deputy mayor. Excellent timing." Louder, he called, "Come in!"

The door opened, and in stepped the last man on earth I wanted to see again.

Eli Carter.

Chapter 2

Eli

I stopped dead in my tracks. *Emma Andrews.* I was so stunned by the sight of her that I let myself do the thing I never let myself do: drink her in.

She hadn't changed much in eight years. Her pale blonde hair was pulled back into a neat and tidy bun, a requirement of her job working with food. When it was down it reached a couple inches past her shoulders—a fact I knew from spotting her at the grocery store two weeks ago. I hadn't let myself look too long then, slipping out of the store before she could see me. I hadn't wanted to ruin her day.

But unless she had suddenly been struck blind, she saw me now. Her day was already ruined, I couldn't do anything about that, so I might as well take what enjoyment I could. I stood there and looked my fill.

Her gray eyes still looked at me like I was all that was wrong with the world. It broke my heart, the way she looked at me. Fair enough, since I had broken hers first. My gaze lingered on her mouth, on her full bottom lip topped by a deep cupid's bow. A kissable mouth that I had always been too afraid to kiss. Back then, losing her friendship, the most important thing in the world to me, wasn't worth the risk.

I should have kissed her. If I could do one thing differently, that would be it. I'd kiss her. Why not? I was always going to lose her anyway.

Two things. If I could do two things differently, I'd go back and kiss her. If I could only change the one thing, I wouldn't have arrested her dad. Not like that, at least. Maybe then the whole kissing thing would have worked itself out.

But I didn't want to think about that mess right now, though it was never far from my mind. I'd save that torture for when I was wide awake at three in the morning. Right now I just wanted to look at her.

Of course, now that she had turned around to face Mayor Whittaker, that meant staring at the back of her head.

"You said the mayor couldn't be otherwise employed by the town. That means *he*"—Emma jerked her head in my direction—"isn't qualified for deputy mayor. He's a police officer."

"Deputy sheriff," I muttered.

"See, and that makes a difference," Mayor Whittaker said. "The mayor can't be otherwise employed by the town, on account of it being a conflict of interest, since the mayor approves the budget and salaries. But Eli isn't directly employed by Hart's Ridge. Technically, he's employed by the county sheriff's office and assigned to Hart's Ridge. We don't even pay his full salary. Thirty grand a year gets us Eli and additional backup as needed."

Emma frowned. Five years ago Hart's Ridge had struck a bargain with the county. At the time, the Hart's Ridge Police Department had cost the town over half a million dollars annually and was by far the biggest line item on the budget. It was a little absurd for a town that averaged three burglaries and zero murders per year. A health clinic and increased spending on education better served the needs of the community than a bloated police force and expanded jail. Emma whole-heartedly supported that decision, a fact

I was very aware of, and so did I. Not that she'd ever believe me if I told her so.

"Secondly," Mayor Whittaker continued, "that requirement is only for *mayor*. There's no such mandate for the deputy mayor."

"That doesn't make any sense!" Emma protested. "He's a police officer—"

"Sheriff's deputy," I corrected again, earning myself an extra glare. Which I kind of enjoyed, to be honest. I preferred her smile, sure, but a glare was better than the big fat nothing she had been serving me for the last eight years.

"A sheriff's deputy can't be deputy mayor," she said firmly. "It's too much power."

"You are a smart cookie, Emma, I always thought so," Mayor Whittaker said. "It's a good point you're making, but facts are facts. I am bound by the ordinances that govern Hart's Ridge and it says right here, in Article I, section two, that the only requirement for deputy mayor is he or she must be at least twenty-five. Could be an oversight; who's to say? Maybe you should look into that, as acting mayor."

Her shoulders started vibrating, a sure sign that her short fuse had reached its limit. I grinned. *That* hadn't changed, either.

As though she felt my smile, and was deeply pissed by it, she whipped her head around to glare at me. That was a mistake on her part. Our gazes locked and held. A jolt of longing hit me in the gut, stealing my breath. I was still trying to take in oxygen when she remembered she was ignoring my existence and turned away again.

My insides ached. I *hated* that. Was I really going to do this, put myself in a position where I had to interact with her daily when she made my insides ache? Hell no.

"Ms. Andrews is right," I said. "It should be someone else. Not me."

Ms. Andrews. I had never called her that, not once in her whole life. We had grown up together, for Chrissake. All I knew was that I couldn't say her name. Much as I liked to pretend I wasn't scared of anything, I knew that wasn't true. I was terrified of the spitfire woman sitting right in front of me. Terrified of what would come out of my mouth if I let myself say her name. Terrified of what she would say in response.

"That's not an option." Mayor Whittaker frowned, first at me, then at Emma. "I'll be honest here. You weren't my first choice, either, Eli, for the very reasons Emma gave. It was pure luck that I happened to look up the ordinance and found the loophole. Times are tough right now, and no one's in a hurry to do free labor. The only thing worse than being an unpaid mayor is being an unpaid deputy mayor. At least the mayor gets to boss people around a bit."

"Then I'll ask again, what makes you think anyone will be eager to take these positions off our hands come July?" she demanded. "What's going to change between now and then?"

"People can't help themselves. It's a human condition. Someone is going to want the power and authority this position holds, even if it doesn't come with a salary. They're going to see you mucking things up and say they can do better."

There was a long pause.

"So you're saying I'm going to muck things up," she said slowly.

The hurt in her voice made me ache again, but I stayed quiet. She didn't want to hear what I had to say.

Mayor Whittaker threw back his head and laughed. "Emma Andrews, I've known you since you were nothing but a baby. You can do anything you set your mind to, maybe not extending to geometry. But here's the truth about being mayor. It doesn't matter how good you do, someone is going to think you're not doing it right, and they can do better. You could do a great job, if you wanted to. But mediocre will do just fine, too."

"Mediocre." Her mouth twisted. "Well, we all know I can do *that*. Okay. I'll be the temporary mayor. But not with him as deputy. Find someone else or I'm out."

She was on her feet now, ready to leave. She turned toward me, and in a moment of weakness I considered standing my ground. There wasn't enough room for us both in the doorway. I wanted her to run into me, bump my shoulder with her own, force me to get out of her way. At the very least tell me to move.

Something.

Anything.

But she didn't want to speak to me or touch me. I knew that, and I was a grown-ass man. I wasn't going to pull her pigtails to get her attention.

I stepped aside.

Then she was gone. And just like before, she didn't look back.

Chapter 3

Emma

Somewhere between my arrival and subsequent departure from Mayor Whittaker's office, the clouds had unified into a single dark mass. Shooting a wary glance upward, I stepped onto the sidewalk...just in time for the sky to unleash a torrential downpour.

I yelped and jumped back under the portico. The rain fell in heavy sheets, so thick I could barely see two feet in front of my face. Now what was I going to do? I had my cell phone with me, of course. I could call Cesar and ask him to come get me. He'd do it, but he'd say *I told you so*. I didn't want to hear *I told you so*. Hadn't I suffered enough for one day?

"You're still here."

I didn't have to turn around to know who was speaking. He had said only a handful of words in Mayor Whittaker's office, but I would recognize his voice anywhere. A deep, quiet voice that made me want to move closer to hear it better. I felt it now, that pull toward him, but I forced myself to stay rooted to the spot.

I didn't respond. I had said everything I needed to say eight years ago, and there wasn't anything to add to that.

The rain was loud enough to dampen the sound of his footsteps, but I felt him move closer. My back tensed and I crossed my arms tightly over my chest. He stopped moving.

"You need a ride?" he asked.

I couldn't ignore a direct question, no matter how much I wanted to. My parents had taught me better than that, and the only thing I hated more than Eli Carter was disappointing my parents. Even if they weren't there to see it. Or maybe *especially* because they weren't here to see it.

But that didn't mean I had to use words. I shook my head, still not looking at him.

There was a long pause. A clap of thunder broke the silence, followed by a sharp crack of lightning.

"Yes, you do," he said matter-of-factly. "It's not clearing up any time soon. You can't wait it out. Even if you run, you're going to get soaked."

All true, but I'd rather be soaked than share space in a car with him even for the five minutes it would take to drive me home.

"And you're wearing a white shirt," he pointed out.

I looked down. Well, damn. My shirt was already see-through in a few places where raindrops had hit me. If I walked home, I'd give the whole neighborhood a show. Main Street had emptied out, but I knew people hadn't gone far. They were sheltering in the shops, staring out the windows, waiting for the rain to pass so they could continue their errands.

"I don't want to," I said. I knew I was whining and I didn't care. Why did the universe hate me?

"I know." The sympathy in his tone annoyed me even more. Why did he have to be so damn *kind*? Didn't he know we were enemies? "Wait here, okay? I'll pull the car around."

"Where would I go?" I said bitterly, throwing my hands out.

He shook his head, smiling slightly, and dashed into the storm. I waited, watching the rain come down. How had life gone upside down? This morning I had been certain of two things: One, I needed to save my business, and two, I was never going to talk to Eli Carter again. A few hours later and here I was, accepting a ride from him, and now I was...mayor?

That couldn't be right.

A black truck pulled up to the sidewalk and honked. I blinked. For some reason, I had been expecting the old red sedan he had driven in high school. But of course he didn't drive that now. That car had already been nearly a decade old when he had inherited it; now it would be ancient.

I ran as fast as I could, rain pelting me with warm, heavy drops the whole way, but it didn't make a bit of difference. I was soaked by the time I reached the door he had pushed open for me.

I slid onto the leather seat...and then kept right on sliding, thanks to my wet body making the seat slick. I fell against him, my lips making awkward contact with his neck. "Oomph," I said against his warm skin.

And for the space of a heartbeat, I pretended things were different.

In the next heartbeat I remembered why they weren't. I sat up, pushing away from him, and wiped the rain from my arms as best I could. It didn't make me feel any less like a drowned squirrel. I shivered.

He turned on the heat, but only cold air blasted out the vents. "It probably won't heat up until I drop you off. You want a blanket? There's one behind your seat."

No, I didn't want to wrap myself in something that smelled like him. I shook my head.

"Suit yourself." He glanced at me and then quickly looked away again. He gripped the steering wheel so tight his knuckles turned white.

"I thought you would have your patrol car," I said. I was glad he didn't.

"I'm off duty." He gestured to his jeans, his eyes never leaving the road. No uniform.

"You don't work Mondays?" I asked, surprised, and then bit my lip, wishing I could take the question back. A question was an invitation to talk, and I didn't want to have a conversation with him.

"No. I requested weekends, and since no one else wanted to be on call for Hart's Ridge, I usually get the shift."

What would make a person give up weekends to work? I *loved* weekends, or the idea of them, anyhow. Everyone having the same two days off as everyone else, so there was nothing better to do than have long, lazy meals capped with an overindulgence of fruity alcoholic beverages? It sounded blissful.

Trouble was, I couldn't *afford* weekends—and neither could most of Hart's Ridge, for that matter. I kept my food truck open seven days a week, six to three, which meant that I started cooking at five a.m. But if I had a choice, I would spend Saturday and Sunday doing absolutely nothing but sleeping in and reading in my hammock.

Yet here was Eli giving it all up. For what? Mondays off? No one liked Mondays. If it were anyone else, my curiosity would have gotten the best of me, and I would have demanded an explanation. But it wasn't anyone else. Eli could work weekends until he died—alone and miserable, because no one went on Monday night dates—for all I cared.

I *didn't* care.

Still, I was curious. I glanced sideways at him. Once I would have claimed that no one knew him better than me. Now I didn't know him at all. He was a mystery.

He didn't even look the same, not really. A man could change a lot between twenty and twenty-eight. Eli certainly had. Back then he'd still had a baby face with a dimple in each cheek. Now he had facial hair, something more than stubble but less than a full-blown beard. I couldn't tell if the dimples were still there underneath. Maybe, maybe not. He'd leaned out and put on muscle over the past eight years, judging from his forearm and the way his gray T-shirt looked on him.

Do not look. Do not look. Do not look.

I hated that I couldn't stop myself.

It was a short drive. He pulled into my long driveway and slowed to a stop. He still didn't look at me.

"Where do you want me to leave you?" he asked. "By the Airstream, or your house?"

It was a fairly large property. The Airstream was parked next to the road, but the house was set a quarter mile farther down the maple-lined drive. It was a big, turreted house left over from the Gilded Age, when it had been a fancy summer home for the Rockefellers. My parents had bought it for nearly nothing when I was still a baby.

The thing had been in shambles, but the bones were good. They had joked about it being their retirement plan. Someday they would turn it into a bed and breakfast. But someday never came, and now I lived there with five extra bedrooms to dust and vacuum. Which I did, even though no one was there to appreciate my work, because the thought of dust bunnies tumbling around gave me hives.

"Here is fine," I said. "It's not three yet. We're still open, even if we don't get any customers."

He leaned forward, resting his forearms on the steering wheel, and peered through the windshield at my Airstream, saying nothing. I followed his gaze, noting the hand-painted wooden sign that simply read *Emma's*, the small gravel parking lot I'd made that replaced a chunk of my lawn, and the picnic table.

"It runs," I said defensively. "I know there are different laws for food trucks than if it were a brick-and-mortar restaurant. It can't be a food truck if it's not mobile. So, it runs."

His lips quirked. "Okay."

"There's no law that says it can't be parked in one place for most of its business hours. There's no law that says I can't own the property it's parked on. It just has to be mobile. And it is. I even haul it to the church on Sundays so people can get coffee and lunch after service."

"I know. I saw you there, once or twice."

"Then why are you eyeballing it like it's a health code violation?" I demanded.

"I'm eyeballing it like I never thought I'd see the day where you hung daisy-printed curtains on your Airstream, but here we are."

"Oh." I was taken aback. "Suzie made them."

"Suzie Barnett? How is she doing?"

The wistfulness in his voice caught me by surprise. Suzie was my best friend. We had all been friends, once—Suzie, Luke Buchanan, Eli, and me—but Suzie had stopped talking to Eli the moment I had. Because I had insisted on it, even though she didn't agree with me. Now Suzie was pregnant with her third baby, but I wasn't feeling particularly generous with that information right now.

"She's fine," I said, not giving him anything more. And feeling a little shitty about it, because I knew Suzie would want me to be better than this. But I wasn't.

"That's good."

Silence fell. I reached for the door handle. It was time to make my escape.

"We need to talk about this," he said.

I shook my head. "No, we don't. There's nothing more to say. Truly."

He made a frustrated noise. "I think there's a lot more to say, actually. Look, I'm not any happier about this than you are. I've got enough on my plate as it is. I don't need to take on the role of deputy mayor, not even for two months. But I don't see as there's a choice, or at least not one my conscience can live with. The Whittakers have served Hart's Ridge for long enough. It's time we did something for them, even if it's just letting them go."

Panic churned my gut. There had to be a way out of this. I couldn't see Eli every day. I just couldn't. A chill ran through me and I rubbed at my arms for warmth. "So what are you saying? We have to work together?"

"I'm saying—" He looked at me and frowned. "For Chrissake. You're freezing to death." He cranked the heat even higher and reached behind the seat, pulled out the blanket I had rejected, and tossed it to me. "I'm saying we don't have to be in a room together to work together. Cell phones? Email? Texting? We have the technology to never see anyone face-to-face again, if that's what we wanted."

"I guess we could try," I said slowly. I huddled under the blanket. It *did* smell good. Like him. Like spicy cologne and cinnamon from the gum he chewed.

"Yeah, we could try. We *should* try. And, listen, if we can't make it work, then we're an embarrassment to our generation and I'll find someone to replace me, even if I have to play dirty to do it. Okay?"

"Okay," I said softly. I couldn't believe I was agreeing to this. But what he said made sense. My feelings didn't matter here. What mattered was helping the Whittakers and helping Hart's Ridge. Or at least keeping the lights on until someone better suited took over.

"So we agree? We're on the same page?"

"Yes."

Thunder rumbled, so close I could feel it in my teeth. I jumped in surprise. "That's not ominous at all," I muttered sarcastically. "Just what we need. In case you haven't noticed, my luck has, historically speaking, completely sucked."

He turned away, obscuring his face in the shadows. "I've noticed."

"But maybe that will work in our favor."

"How so?"

I shrugged. "What I'm saying is that I expect this all to go sideways sooner or later, but I'm used to that. I don't really know what to do with myself when things are going right. So maybe bad luck...maybe bad luck is exactly what we need."

He offered a small grin. "I can work with that. My luck hasn't been the best, either."

"So...I won't see you tomorrow, but you can text me, and I won't ignore you. You need my number?"

"Has it changed?"

"Nope."

"Then I don't need it."

I didn't know what to say to that. Nobody memorized phone numbers anymore. Was I still saved in his contact list? I had deleted him, but I hadn't blocked him. I'd known then that I wouldn't need to. Eli was a man who took a woman at her word. If a woman said don't call, he wasn't going to call.

I pushed off the blanket, opened the car door, and darted out into the rain. Something made me pause and turn back. He was watching me, making sure I got in safely. That was Eli, down to the bone. Always making sure I was safe, even if safety came with a broken heart and a dad in prison.

A mess of emotions rioted inside me. Love, loss, heartbreak, hope, rage. *Rage.* I focused on it, let it grow and crystallize until it drove out everything else. Rage was easier to deal with than all the other emotions. At least, I knew what to do with it.

"I'll never forgive you, Eli Carter!" I shouted.

It turned out there was something left to say, after all—if only because I was in danger of forgetting it myself.

Chapter 4

Eli

I let out a slow breath as Emma disappeared inside the Airstream and slammed the door shut. Then I sat there, too stunned to move, much less drive.

The image of her standing there in the rain, her white shirt entirely transparent and clinging to her breasts and pale lilac bra, was seared into my brain. She had looked so wild, so touchable, so *Emma*. And then she had hurled those words like a grenade.

I'll never forgive you, Eli Carter.

"Yeah, well, that makes two of us," I muttered to myself. I threw my truck in reverse and got the hell out of there.

The dashboard clock read one o'clock. My stomach rumbled, reminding me that I hadn't eaten lunch yet. I was half-tempted to turn back and get a burrito. She needed the money, I needed the food. Everyone claimed Cesar's burritos were amazing. I had never experienced one firsthand, knowing I wasn't a welcome customer.

I *still* wasn't welcome. No way in hell would Emma cook me a burrito, unless it was laced with arsenic. Anyway, it was a Monday—my day off—and that meant lunch with my friend Luke. It was our weekly tradition for the past several years, me eating while Luke tended bar.

I pulled up to Goat's Tavern, a couple miles from the bustle of Main Street. It was a ramshackle-looking, wood-beamed barn, but like everything Luke Buchanan created, it was built to last. Behind the tavern was the 1860s farmhouse, passed down from one Buchanan to another over several generations, where Luke lived and rented rooms to thru-hikers. There were also a couple cabins, relics of the migrants who had once worked the land.

There weren't more than two or three cars in the parking lot, but I knew the place would be packed. Hart's Ridge was only ten miles off the Appalachian Trail, and we were at peak season. Word of mouth had made Goat's Tavern a popular stop off, where hikers could get a shower, a hot meal, and a comfortable bed for the night. On a day like today, with the sky dumping buckets of water, it was a sure bet that hikers would be holed up here.

The rain was still coming down with no sign of letting up, and I got slightly soaked in the couple steps from my truck to the front door. I wiped the water from my face and looked around warily.

"Where's Goat?" I asked. The little devil could be anywhere. Sneaking up on people was his specialty. Still, he hated thunderstorms, so he was probably hiding.

"He's—" Luke started. The phone rang and he held up his finger to indicate it would be a minute while simultaneously picking up the receiver. "Goat's Tavern." There was a pause. "Yeah. Where you at?" Another pause. "Okay, hold on a minute." He set the phone on the bar. "Hey, Ethan, we've got another hiker."

"On it." Ethan, his younger brother, picked up the phone. "What's your mile marker?"

Luke turned back to me. "Goat's in my office. Pooping on everything, probably, but what am I gonna do about it? You know he hates being outside when it's storming. So what can I get you?"

"Burger, medium, sweet potato fries." I didn't even hesitate. My order rarely changed.

"Coming right up." Luke shouted the order to the kitchen. He grabbed a glass from behind the bar. "You want the Blue Moon? We still have it on tap."

I shook my head. When it came to alcohol, I had a firm rule, born from a decade of watching my dad drink his life away after Mom left: sadness and alcohol didn't mix. I could drink when I wanted to have a good time, or when I wanted to relax after a long, hard day. But never, ever to mask sadness. And right now, I wasn't feeling exactly jovial. "Root beer today."

Luke paused with his hand on the beer pull, studied me for a moment, then reversed course toward the soda fountain. "Rough morning?" he asked over his shoulder.

I didn't answer right away. Luke might look like a rough-and-tumble mountain man, from his shaggy hair to his worn flannel with the sleeves rolled up to his elbows, but I knew better. Luke Buchanan could out gossip any fourteen-year-old girl.

But he was also a good friend. And once upon a time, he had been a good friend to Emma, too. If anyone could understand the horrifying predicament I now found myself in, it was Luke.

I looked right, then left. I checked the mirror above the wall of liquor to see the restaurant behind me. About a dozen or so people, all strangers. No one I recognized. I leaned forward.

"You know the Whittakers are moving out?" I asked.

Luke slid me the glass of root beer. "Yeah, man. Mayor Whittaker even asked me to step in for him. Asked Ethan to be deputy."

"He asked you to be mayor?"

Luke laughed. "He asked every Hart's Ridge resident over the age of twenty-five, near as I can tell. Don't think he's having much luck finding someone."

"Oh, he found someone all right."

"Oh, yeah? Who's the lucky sucker? It can't be you. You're a cop."

"Emma Andrews."

"Huh." He mulled that over. "Interesting choice."

"No, the interesting part is he made me deputy mayor."

Luke's eyebrows shot up and he let out a low whistle. "No shit. Seriously?"

"Yeah."

"But you two have history. *Bad* history."

I raised my glass in a sardonic toast. "I'm aware."

Luke was quiet. "Food's up!" came a voice from the kitchen. Luke disappeared through the swinging door, then reappeared and set the plate down in front of me.

Thank God. I was starving. I took a huge bite of the burger and nodded appreciatively.

"So." Luke leaned casually against the counter, his blue eyes deceptively wide and innocent. "What does Claire think about all this? About you working side by side with Emma?"

I couldn't answer with my mouth full of burger, so I settled for a lethal glare. Claire Miller was my girlfriend. She lived in Piedmont, the next town over.

I finished chewing, took a swig of root beer, and said, "Claire doesn't know anything about it. For one, because I never told her about Emma. That's all ancient history that Claire doesn't need to know about, seeing as Emma hadn't said one word to me in eight years until today. And for two, I'm ending things with Claire, so it doesn't much matter what she thinks about it anyway."

"Huh. When did you decide that? I thought things were going well with you and her."

"Been thinking about it for a while," I said. "She and I are both busy. It was hard to make time to see each other."

All true. We were both busy, and the kicker was I wasn't sure I cared. But my ambivalence toward Claire had become painfully sharp when I saw Emma soaked by the rain. There was nothing ambivalent about *those* feelings. Love and sex don't have to go hand-in-hand, but it was a completely different thing having those feelings for someone when you didn't have them for your girlfriend.

Luke cocked his head, looking at me. "What's it been now? Six months?"

"Four."

"Right." Luke grinned. "It's always four."

My brow furrowed. "What's that supposed to mean?"

"It means that you don't do casual dating, but you don't do serious either. You get exclusive with someone immediately, and then four months later, you're done. No holidays either, I've noticed."

"I was with Claire on Easter." I dipped a fry in ketchup and popped it in my mouth.

Luke snorted. "That doesn't count. I mean holidays like Thanksgiving. Christmas. Valentine's Day. You don't do those."

"Coincidence."

"Nah. You just don't want to get serious, and holidays are serious."

"Maybe I don't want to get serious because I haven't met the girl I want to get serious with. Did you ever think of that?"

"I did think of that, as it so happens, and do you know what I decided?"

I eyed him over the rim of my soda. "Any chance you decided it was high time you minded your own damn business?"

"No."

I sighed. "I didn't think so."

"The problem isn't that you haven't found the girl you want to get serious with. It's that you think you *have* but she wants nothing to do with you."

I wasn't about to ask who Luke was talking about. *Emma.* There was no one else. Luke had been around when everything went down, and he knew how things were now between us now. But he also knew how things were *before*, because he was there for that, too. He knew how I had felt about her before everything went to shit.

That didn't make him right, though. I couldn't deny I felt some kind of way about Emma, but I had never put much stock into the idea of soul mates or one true love. True, I hadn't fallen in love with anyone since Emma, but that didn't mean I couldn't. I just hadn't met her yet.

"I'm not going to dignify that with a reply."

Luke grinned. "I don't need dignity, man. I'm beneath that."

"At least you're self-aware." I raised my burger. "Food is good today."

"Yeah, Priscilla is amazing." Luke braced his arms on the counter and leaned forward. "So."

I raised my eyebrows. "So?"

"So you're really going to do this? Work side by side, every damn day, with a woman you're in love with who happens to hate your guts?"

I paused. *In love*...that wasn't the right phrase at all. I felt something for her, of course I did. How could I not? Even eight years later, it was still Emma. But I didn't know her, not the way I did then. You had to know someone to be in love. A lot could change in eight years. What if she had developed an affinity for collecting dolls? Dolls were creepy as hell. I definitely couldn't be in love with some psycho doll collector.

"I'm not in love with her. We have history. There's a difference. Anyway, we have an arrangement. We're going to use strictly virtual communication. Emails and texts, since she probably doesn't even want to hear my voice. Nothing face-to-face."

"Right," Luke said dubiously.

"It's going to work. Two months, that's it. What could possibly go wrong?"

"I guess. I mean, she couldn't possibly hate you any more than she does now, right?"

I choked on a French fry. "Right," I gasped.

She couldn't. Could she?

Chapter 5

Emma

"Emma Andrews, what in the world are you doing?" said a laughing voice from above me.

I was lying flat on my back on the living room floor. Beneath me was the braided rug my great-great-grandma had made from scraps of clothes and blankets when she had been no older than I was now. Above me the ceiling fan spun lazy circles. It was something I had done since I was a young child. I didn't have a good reason for why. It soothed me, though.

Strategic regrouping, Dad called it. It was cute Dad had that much faith in me. There was nothing strategic about it.

"Go away, Suzie," I said. "I'm having a moment."

"This moment is unbecoming of your new station in life," came another voice, also laughing. At my expense, knowing my friends.

I lifted my head, craning my neck until I saw Kate Gonzales half hidden behind Suzie's ever-expanding belly. "I take it you heard the news."

"We ran into Cesar at the hardware store. He gave us the whole story."

I groaned. When Eli had dropped me off, I had stormed into the Airstream full of righteous anger and looking like a hot mess. Cesar had taken one look at me and thrown me an apron to cover myself up. That was when I had realized Eli had seen *everything*. It put my dramatic exit in an embarrassing new light.

That part, Cesar probably hadn't shared. At least, I hoped not.

But the part where I had informed him that I had been conscripted as mayor and he had promptly laughed himself sick, yes, that part was fair game. The only question was how he had managed to stop laughing long enough to get the story out.

"Then you understand why I'm on the floor," I said. "It's the only way I can be sure the ground won't sink into a pit of quicksand beneath me."

Suzie nudged my ribs with her sandaled toe. "Stop being dramatic and get up."

"No." I closed my eyes and waited for them to give up.

No such luck.

"If she won't come to us, we'll just have to go to her," Suzie said. "Oh my *God*, the ground is so far away. You're going to help me back up, right?"

My eyes shot open in alarm as Suzie and Kate joined me on the floor, sandwiching me between them. Suzie grunted as she landed, and the hundred-year-old pine floorboards groaned, making Kate giggle.

"Shut up," Suzie groused. "When you did this, you were seventeen. Pregnancy is different in your late twenties, let me tell you."

Kate rolled her eyes. "Oh, please. You have a decade of baby-making years ahead of you. You're not old."

"I *feel* old. And large, in an unbalanced sort of way."

"Well," Kate said comfortingly, "that's because you *are* large in an unbalanced sort of way."

I cleared my throat. "Can we get back to the purpose of this ambush, which is that I am now mayor of Hart's Ridge and we are all doomed?"

"We're not doomed," Suzie said. "At least, no more so than normal. Things aren't great right now, but that's not your fault. No one can blame you for the processing plant closing."

Suzie steadfastly refused to call it the chicken plant, like everyone else did. This was because she kept hens in her backyard and loved every single one of them, so much so that she had named them after Jane Austen characters.

I couldn't help smiling a little before remembering that there was nothing to smile about. I sighed. "No, it's not my fault. But now it's my responsibility."

I squeezed my eyes shut again in a futile attempt to block out reality. More responsibility was the last thing I needed. My life was already too full of it, and it had been that way from the moment of Mom's cancer diagnosis.

Once upon a time I had been a normal middle-class kid. My dad taught chemistry at the University of North Carolina, and my mom was a third-grade teacher at Hart's Ridge Elementary. We weren't rich, but we could afford to spend summer vacations driving around national parks in the Airstream.

All that had changed when Mom got sick.

Stage II cervical cancer. At first we had thought she would be okay. Survival rates weren't in the nineties like with Stage I, but the odds were better than a coin toss. But I had never won a coin toss in my life, and Mom didn't win against cancer.

It had taken five years of surgeries and chemotherapy before it killed her. Five years of me doing my best to take care of her while she slowly wasted away. I raced home every day after school—and sometimes skipped classes altogether—to make sure Mom was comfortable. I washed her hair, made sure she took her meds, did all the cooking and cleaning. I helped her go to the bathroom, and when even that was too much, I changed the bedpan. Dad helped when he could, but for the most part I was on my own. Losing his job would mean losing health insurance.

Even with health insurance, once the bills started coming, they didn't stop. The stress affected everything. Dad wasn't tenured, and then he was laid off. But the bills kept coming and they didn't stop until she died.

But by then he had found a way to put that chemistry knowledge to use.

With Mom's death and Dad's arrest, I traded responsibility of one parent for another. Dropping out of community college to work full time was the only way to cover the mortgage and the defense bills.

Being responsible for my parents was terrible, draining, stressful—and those were the people I loved most in the world. Now I was responsible for the whole damn town, and I wasn't sure I loved more than a handful of *them*.

"I know it's overwhelming," Kate said. "We're here to help."

That made me feel marginally better, even though I suspected that their "help" would mostly consist of listening to me bitch and moan. They weren't any more qualified to be mayor than I was. Suzie was a stay-at-home mom of two with a third baby on the way, and Kate ran a candy shop. Neither of them knew anything about being mayor.

I was screwed, all right. The whole town was screwed.

"You don't have to do this alone," Suzie said. "Of course we'll help. Who is replacing Mrs. Whittaker as deputy mayor?"

My stomach twisted. Other than shouting *I'll never forgive you, Eli Carter!* his name hadn't crossed my lips in eight years. The look on his face when I said it was the same as it had been all those years ago. Resignation, sadness, and something else that was neither of those things. Something she was afraid to give a name to, because it felt like a punch to the chest.

"Eli Carter," I said. "Because the universe hates me."

"No!" Suzie gasped. "Are you serious?"

"What's wrong with Eli Carter?" Kate asked. "He seems like a solid choice. Maybe a little taciturn and serious, but he's also, you know, *hot*. I guess that's not a requirement for deputy mayor, but maybe it should be."

In unison, Suzie and I turned to give her incredulous looks.

"What?" Kate asked defensively. "What's with the looks? He *is* hot! All broody and those *muscles*."

I covered my face and let out a muffled shriek.

"Eli Carter isn't hot. We hate him." Suzie paused, considering. "Well, maybe he is a little hot. But he's also the officer who arrested Emma's dad. How do you not know? You've lived in Hart's Ridge your entire life! It was huge news."

Kate side-eyed us. "Gee, I don't know. Maybe because we didn't know each other very well back then? Or maybe because I was neck-deep in my own grief and dealing with a daughter who didn't understand why her daddy was never coming home again."

I winced. When my own life fell apart eight years ago, so had Kate's. We hadn't been close friends back then. Kate was only two years older than me, but we had gone to different schools our entire lives. I had gone to the local public schools, but Kate's family, one of the wealthiest in Hart's Ridge, sent her to private school in Piedmont.

I had known *of* Kate, of course. Gossip travelled fast between the two schools, so everyone knew about the pregnant senior. Kate had married her boyfriend, George, right after graduation, the day after her eighteenth birthday. George had joined the Army and was immediately deployed to the Middle East. Four years later, while stationed in California for training, he had stopped to help someone change their tire on the side of the road and was hit by a car. Leaving Kate to raise their daughter, Jessica, alone.

"Fair enough," Suzie said hastily.

"Sorry," I muttered. "See? I'm too self-centered to be mayor."

Kate snorted. "Right. Because the news shows us so many humble, generous politicians as examples."

"You make a good point."

"So back to Eli Carter. What's the story?"

"Well, you already know that eight years ago, after her mom died and her dad got laid off, Emma's dad was arrested for making meth with the intention to distribute it."

I gritted my teeth. That was the charge, and it was technically accurate. *Technically*. But it wasn't the *truth*, in my opinion. It wasn't like my dad was hanging on street corners, making deals. He was the dealer's source. Like...like a marijuana farmer, except he was a meth cooker.

That was how I explained it to myself. Because even though I knew that cooking meth wasn't at all the same as growing weed, he was my *dad*. And he had reasons. Good reasons. Maybe I was being too soft, and maybe there wasn't really any excuse for what he did, but I loved him. Despite everything.

Kate nodded. "Go on."

"Back then, Emma and Eli were..." Suzie hesitated. She looked at me. "Do you want to tell it?"

I shook my head. "I really, really don't."

"Okay. So back then, Emma and Eli were really close. They had been friends since, like, kindergarten. All three of us, and Luke, were friends in high school, but they were practically married."

"We were not!" I yelled. "We never even went on a date. We were just friends."

"Sure, whatever," Suzie said in a tone that implied the opposite. "Anyway, after high school, Emma went to community college and Eli joined the police force. When she came home for the summer, she discovered what her dad was up to. She confided in Eli, and he betrayed her. He arrested her dad."

"Oh my God." Kate's eyes went wide as she digested this. "It's like a soap opera. But holy crap, Emma, why did you tell a *police officer* your dad was cooking meth?"

"We were friends. *Best* friends," I protested. "I didn't know who else to turn to and he was...he was *Eli*. He was always the person I went to. I thought maybe he could help because helping was what he did. Always. It's not like I walked into the police station and filed a report. He wasn't even on duty. I never thought he would arrest my dad."

I bit my lip. That was true, wasn't it? I hadn't thought he would arrest my dad? It didn't feel like a lie, exactly. Just...wrong, somehow. It was the truth, but maybe not the whole truth. The whole truth was buried in a deep, dark corner of my soul. If I shined a light there, what would I find? I didn't want to know. Couldn't *bear* to know.

This much was true, at least: I loved my dad. When he was sentenced to eight years in prison, my life was turned upside down. That was Eli's fault. And I would never forgive him for it.

"So what now?" Kate asked. "How are you two going to run this town together when we hate his guts?"

We. I appreciated that. Kate might enjoy a nice set of muscles, but she was nothing if not loyal.

"We made a deal. Communication will be one-hundred percent virtual. Texting, email, phone calls if we absolutely have to. Nothing face-to-face." I lifted my fist, Scarlett O'Hara style.

"As God is my witness, I will never see Eli Carter again."

Chapter 6

Eli

The problem with making plans was that the universe had no qualms breaking them for you.

I had been so sure that we could do this, that between modern technology and sheer stubbornness we could make this crazy arrangement work. So when Mrs. Whittaker called me early the next morning and asked me to meet her at City Hall, of course I had said yes.

We needed to go over the basic housekeeping matters, such as getting me a badge and key to the building, passwords for the computer systems, and that sort of thing. Not to mention what the job of deputy mayor actually entailed, because I didn't have a clue. As far as I knew,

Mrs. Whittaker shook a lot of hands, kissed some babies, and...baked pies? There had to be more to it than that.

I hoped so, anyway. I wasn't really the baby-kissing type. Although I did make a damn good apple pie.

I had figured I would meet with Mrs. Whittaker, get everything squared away, and text Emma after to give her the rundown. I was completely unprepared to hear Mrs. Whittaker say, "We'll just wait for Emma and Thomas so we can get started."

I blinked. "Come again?" I said, just to be sure. There must have been some mistake.

"Emma and Thomas. He's getting her badge taken care of right now, but they should be back any minute. No point in going over everything twice, is there?"

"I figured you would get me set up, and Mr. Whittaker would take care of Emma. Separately."

Mrs. Whittaker laughed. "Don't be silly. You will be working together, won't you? Might as well start now. Anyway, it makes sense to do you both in one go."

"I—"

"Yes?" Mrs. Whittaker looked at me expectantly.

I looked at her kind face and lost my nerve. I couldn't tell her that Emma regarded me as a mortal enemy, and that she would rather shave her head than be in the same room with me. I couldn't tell her we had made a deal to conduct all our business dealings virtually.

If I told her all that, Mrs. Whittaker might decide they couldn't leave after all, and the grandkids would have to wait another few years—if they lived that long. The Whittakers weren't exactly young, and Mr. Whittaker had a minor heart attack a year ago.

I couldn't have that on my conscience. My conscience had taken enough of a beating as it was.

"I think that's a good idea," I finished lamely. "We'll do it together."

Mrs. Whittaker beamed. "Wonderful."

Emma wouldn't agree. No, Emma was going to kill me. Physically. None of this emotional warfare she had employed yesterday. She didn't like firearms, but she struck me as the type to always have a pocketknife handy. She would have to get close enough to me to use it, though. Maybe even touch me, as much as she would hate that. She might put her hand on my shoulder, catch me off guard. I didn't want to be stabbed, so I'd have to find a way to disarm her without hurting her. We might have to wrestle...

"Are you all right, Eli?" Mrs. Whittaker asked. "You look a little flushed."

I jerked to attention. What the hell was the matter with me? I was sitting in the deputy mayor's office, my dick half hard, fantasizing about a wrestling match with my ex-best friend. I was sick in the head. If Emma ever knew the turn my thoughts took, she would kill me twice.

The trouble was, there had been a distinct lack of sex in my life for far too long. Of *good* sex, that is. Claire and I had managed to get naked usually twice a month, but it had been...well, the word *placid* came to mind, and that wasn't a word that should have anything to do with sex. Placid rhymed with flaccid.

I was pretty sure Claire agreed with me on that, because when I had called her up last night to suggest we meet for coffee, she had sighed. That was when I knew things were truly over between us, but then she had followed it up with asking if maybe we could just break up over the phone, no hard feelings, because it was such a long drive.

I don't know if I was more relieved or insulted. The whole thing was over in three minutes—a new record for me. Not that I'd tell Luke that.

So it wasn't that I needed to wrestle Emma, per se. I needed sex. No way would sex with Emma be placid. It couldn't be, because nothing about the way we felt for each other was calm or quiet.

I shifted uncomfortably on the vinyl-padded chair. "It's a little warm in here."

Mrs. Whittaker nodded apologetically. "It's an old building. No air conditioning, but the ceiling fans work and the windows open. Still, you're bound to feel the heat when temperatures get into the nineties, like today. Fortunately, we don't have many of those days." She frowned, giving me an accusing stare as though I were personally responsible. "More than we had in *my* day, though."

Put me right in my place. "Oh."

"There's never enough money for those kinds of projects, it seems. We—oh, here they are now. Goodness, what happened to you?" Mrs. Whittaker exclaimed. "Thomas, you're a mess."

I turned in my chair to see what she was referring to. Mr. Whittaker was, in fact, a mess. His suit jacket was slung over one arm, and his face was red and dripping sweat.

"Elevators are out. Had to walk...six flights of stairs," Mr. Whittaker panted. He made a beeline for the fan in the corner of the office, revealing Emma behind him. "Oof, that's better. The stairwell was hot as Hades."

"You should have gone slower, Thomas," Mrs. Whittaker scolded, her forehead knit in a worried frown. "Doctor O'Hare warned you not to overexert yourself. Should I call her?"

"I'm fine, I'm fine," Mr. Whittaker said, waving her off.

Watching them, I was surer than ever that we were doing the right thing. Mr. Whittaker needed to retire for the sake of his health. I glanced at Emma, wondering if she'd come to the same realization.

Emma didn't look messy—she looked *mussed*. Like...like she had been wrestling for control of a pocketknife. Her cheeks were glowing pink and her skin was glistening. Tiny blonde whisps had escaped her bun to frame her face like a halo. A bolt of lust socked me in the gut, followed quickly by annoyance. This was my punishment for those pervy thoughts earlier. How was I supposed to keep from touching her when she kept looking so...touchable?

I growled at the unfairness of it all and everyone turned to look at me.

"It's—it's not right that City Hall is in such bad shape," I said, covering my thoughts. "It's one of the oldest buildings in Hart's Ridge. It should be a source of pride."

Mrs. Whittaker gave me a bemused look. "It's wonderful to see you so...erm...passionate about our historical buildings, Eli. I'm sure you'll think of some way to help during your tenure as deputy mayor. I feel so much better leaving the town in your hands, now that I see how strongly you feel about Hart's Ridge."

"Don't know how you'll fix up the place, seeing as we're short on funds," Mr. Whittaker broke in. "We're always short on funds. You'll learn to say *no* a lot in the next two months."

Mrs. Whittaker glared at him briefly, then smiled again at Emma and me. "He's not wrong. There's never enough money for anything, it seems. Perhaps you could hold a bake sale," she added brightly.

"A...a bake sale," I repeated, dumbfounded. If the financial future of Hart's Ridge rested on my ability to convince neighbors to buy baked goods, we were screwed. I glanced sideways at Emma, who was looking everywhere but at me. I sighed. "Sure, why not."

"And there's always the Fourth of July celebration. Maybe you could hold a raffle to raise the funds to renovate City Hall," Mrs. Whittaker said.

At the mention of the Fourth of July celebration, Emma's head snapped up. "The celebration?"

"You know about the celebration, Emma," Mrs. Whittaker said, frowning slightly. "It happens every year. Fireworks, a Ferris wheel, food. This year is extra special because it's the hundred-and-fiftieth anniversary of the founding of Hart's Ridge."

"I mentioned it to you yesterday, remember?" Mr. Whittaker interjected. "Permits and such."

"Yes, but—" Emma looked at me for the first time since entering the room, her gray eyes full of panic. "But I thought..."

Aw, hell.

Whether she liked it or not, I was backing her up. Always. I cleared my throat. "I feel like this was maybe a bit downplayed when we agreed to take on these positions."

The Whittakers exchanged guilty looks.

"The thing is, we would love to stay. The Fourth of July celebration is one of our favorite events. But Thomas's health won't allow it." Mrs. Whittaker shook her head firmly. "The stress of planning an event like this is simply too much. Our house sold much faster than we thought it would, and we took that for a sign. It's time for us to go."

I couldn't argue with that. The chair squeaked as I stood. "Will you excuse us for a moment? Ms. Andrews, step into the hallway with me for a minute, if you don't mind."

Judging from the look she shot me, she minded a whole lot, but she nodded and followed me out of the office. The moment the door shut behind them, she whirled on her toes to confront me.

"You said we wouldn't have to see each other!" she hissed in a loud whisper. "It's not even twenty-four hours later and here we are, seeing each other."

I rubbed the back of my neck sheepishly. "We might have to amend our arrangement. There's no way we can put together this kind of event without spending some time in the same room."

She crossed her arms, eyes narrowed. "How *much* time?"

All the time. I wanted all the time. But she wasn't going to give me that. And after eight years, I shouldn't care. But I did. I was a fucking masochist for this girl.

"An hour. Let's say we meet for an hour every Wednesday. That's it."

"An hour? That's it?"

"An hour. Not a second longer, I promise. We might not even need to keep meeting after the first few times. We just need to hit the ground running."

"An hour on Wednesdays." She pursed her lips. "Tomorrow is Wednesday."

"Right." I held my breath, waiting.

It seemed like forever until she finally said, "Then I guess I'll see you tomorrow."

Chapter 7

Emma

I woke up feeling unsettled. No surprise, when my life had gone topsy-turvy in the space of forty-eight hours. The realization that my income was drying up, the new and entirely unwanted responsibility of being mayor of Hart's Ridge, and the abrupt end of eight years of giving my best-friend-turned-enemy the silent treatment—any one of those things on its own was enough to knock me on my backside, but the onslaught of everything all at once was too much.

I had told Eli that I was used to bad luck. Hell, I was even *good* at it. I was a worrier by nature, and I found that if I worried long enough and hard enough, the solution was bound to appear.

But this...*this* was different. And it was all Eli's fault. I could worry about my food truck, and maybe I would figure something out, as Cesar had said. I could worry about being mayor, and maybe I could find my way out of that, too. But Eli...I could worry about Eli until the sun imploded, and it wouldn't make one bit of difference. He would still exist. He would still make my insides churn and my heart beat faster and my body lean closer, as if those eight years hadn't been more than eight seconds.

And *that* was unsettling.

So I did what I always did when I felt unsettled, which was to visit my father in the Asheville Prison.

The guard looked slightly surprised to see me when I arrived. I gave him a reassuring nod. My normal visiting hours were every other Saturday, at five p.m., and of course Christmas and his birthday. It was unlike me to show up on a Wednesday morning, because most mornings I would be slammed with customers at the food truck. Not a problem, right now. Cesar was once again covering the shift and probably reading a book out of sheer boredom.

The guard showed me to the visiting room, where there was a small table and a chair on either side. The first few times I had visited, there had been a glass partition separating us and we communicated by phone. Since then, Dad had earned privileges for good behavior. We couldn't hold hands, but we could hug hello and goodbye.

A minute later Dad appeared—without handcuffs, because he had been deemed nonviolent—looking much better than he ever had before his arrest. Back then, he had lost too much weight from worry and there had been dark puffy pouches beneath his eyes from lack of sleep. Now he looked rested and healthy. He liked to say that there were only two things to do in prison: work out and read books, and he did both of those in spades.

After a quick hug, we sat down opposite each other, hands clasped politely on the table in front of us, not touching. Dad was always so careful to follow the rules. In his lifetime, he had only ever broken the one. A major one, but still. Just one. That was all it took, apparently. The system was unforgiving that way.

"It's Wednesday. You never come on Wednesdays. What's going on, Emma-bear?" he asked, using his old nickname for me.

It had come about when I was a toddler, not because I was as cute and cuddly as a teddy bear, but because when I didn't get my way, I would shake my fists and growl as ferociously as a toddler could.

Oh no, my baby is a bear! What will I dooooo? my mother would mock wail.

Good times, in retrospect.

"Everything, Dad. Everything is going on." I swallowed hard. Of course he knew that the processing plant was closing, but when I had seen him last, there had still been hope—and customers. Maybe a senator would step in, or the governor. But that hadn't happened and it was clear now that no miracle was coming. Lord knew the mayor wasn't going to produce a last-minute Hail Mary.

The mayor being me was a solid guarantee on that.

"Tell me about it," he said, in that Dad way he had, the way that made me want to do exactly that.

The whole story came pouring out. That I hadn't had more than a dozen customers all week. That my last hope was high-tailing it out of town and leaving me in charge. That I somehow had to find a way to save the food truck, save the town, *and* plan the Fourth of July celebration. That Eli—

And there I stopped short.

Dad's eyebrows shot up to his slightly receding hairline. "Eli? Eli Carter? What about him?"

I chewed my lip. To be honest, I had no idea how my dad felt about Eli. We never talked about him. I could only imagine that if I hated Eli, my dad felt that ten times more.

He had known Eli since we were kids. Watched him grow up. And then been arrested by him. That didn't exactly inspire fond feelings, I figured.

"He's acting deputy mayor," I said finally.

"Is he? Kind of an odd choice, given his profession." He tilted his head, considering. "Well, it could be worse. Eli's a good kid."

Not a kid. Kids didn't have scruffy jaws that made her wonder...*things*...and shoulders that stretched tee shirts to their limits. Kids didn't—I gave myself a mental slap. *Bad Emma*.

"Dad, he arrested you," I protested.

"I'm aware."

"I can't work with him."

"You *can*. You mean you won't. There's a difference."

I growled in annoyance.

Dad laughed. "Emma-bear, don't you go holding grudges on my account. I can hold my own grudges just fine, thank you. In the case of Eli Carter, I choose not to hold a grudge."

That surprised me, but maybe it shouldn't have. Dad was always kind, above all else.

"I have a lot of anger," he continued. "I'm angry at cancer. I'm angry at a system that made it so easy for a middle-class, hard-working family to lose everything in the blink of an eye—and by that I mean paying hospital bills, not putting me in jail. I'm mad at myself most of all. But Eli was just doing his job, honey. I can't be angry at that."

I crossed my arms over my chest. "Well, *I* can," I huffed.

Because if I didn't...well, if I couldn't blame Eli then there was only one person left. *Me*. I had never told my dad the truth of that night, that I had been the one who had told Eli. What would he say if he knew? He might forgive Eli, but could he forgive his own daughter? That was a much deeper betrayal.

"So what are you going to do?" he asked. "Let the town fall down around our ears for the sake of pride and vengeance? This isn't a Greek tragedy. Don't make it end like one."

"Fine. No launching a war to destroy my enemies."

He laughed, and I knew I had pleased him with that reference. He would love nothing better than a daughter who could discuss the themes and subtexts of Greek literature. Unfortunately, that was not me. I had never read Greek literature in my life, even when it was assigned in school. I had, however, seen *Troy*, on account of the hot, naked men.

"So what's the plan, Emma?" he asked. "You always have a plan."

"Not this time." I hesitated. "Maybe if I do a bad enough job of it, someone else will realize they can do better. Someone who knows how to balance budgets and plan events and all that kind of stuff that mayors do. I can't do any of that." I looked at him helplessly. "What am I supposed to do, Dad? How am I supposed to help? I'm the least qualified mayor ever."

"I don't know anything more about being mayor than you do, honey. But I do know this. Whenever I'm lost, I think of that thing your mom used to say. Do you remember?"

I remembered.

"Leave it better than you found it," I whispered.

He nodded. "That's right. Leave it better than you found it. That advice has never steered me wrong. Maybe you won't be mayor for more than sixty days. Maybe you don't know how to do the job they've asked you to do. All right. You can still leave it better than you found it. Just one thing, Emma. One small, tiny thing."

One small, tiny thing. Yes, even I could do that. I had never been able to fix big things, not for lack of trying. Mom's cancer. Dad's highly illegal side business. But a small thing, maybe I could fix that. I could leave Hart's Ridge better than I found it, in one small, tiny way, at least.

But what?

I parked my truck outside Dreamer's Cafe. I was ten minutes late to meet Eli. I was never late to anything, but I was late now, for the simple reason that this was the last place on Earth I wanted to be.

Usually I would be thrilled to have lunch at Dreamer's. It was, hands down, the best food Hart's Ridge had to offer, even over Cesar's burritos—a belief I would take to my grave, because Cesar would never speak to me again if I said it out loud. Dreamer's was a brilliant fusion of standard American fare and Salvadoran flavors—kind of like Hart's Ridge itself. There was a large population of first, second, and third generation immigrants from El Salvador and Guatemala here in Hart's Ridge.

My mouth watered as I imagined biting into a lamb burger with a side of yuca fries. It could all be mine, but I had to suffer through an hour or two of Eli's company to get it.

I stepped down from my truck but I didn't go in. Not yet. I stood on the sidewalk, keys jingling in my hand, my brain pinging between the two alternatives. *Yuca fries.* Run away. *Yuca fries.* Run away.

My stomach rumbled. Yuca fries won out.

Before I could talk myself out of it, I shoved my keys in my bag and strode into the restaurant. Delmy Garcia, the owner, nodded at me. "He's over there. The table by the window."

"Thanks."

I looked to where Delmy had indicated. My throat tightened. He was there, all right, and this time in uniform. I knew he hadn't done it purposefully to remind me of who he was—he was on duty, after all—but that uniform was all I could see. In that uniform, he wasn't Eli, my onetime best friend. He was Eli, Arrester of Fathers.

Crossing the room was awkward with him watching every step I took, and somehow it made me forget what I was supposed to do with my arms. By the time I made it to the table, my body felt like it had too many elbows and knees.

"Hey," I said.

He half stood from his chair, waiting for me to take my seat before he sat down again. So damn polite. "Hey. I wasn't sure you would come."

"I said I would, didn't I?" I said defensively, as if I hadn't been on the verge of chickening out just a minute ago.

"Yeah, and then you stood there on the sidewalk for a good five minutes looking like you would rather have all your teeth pulled."

Busted. I didn't blush, because I wasn't embarrassed. Why should I be? I hadn't arrested *his* dad—who, once upon a time, had a terrible habit of driving drunk, before ultimately dying in a drunk driving crash with a light pole. At the time, Eli had said that at least his dad had waited until his eighteenth birthday to orphan him, unlike his mother. Eli's sense of humor had always run pretty dark. Technically, though, Eli wasn't an orphan. He just didn't know where his mother was.

Or did he? Had she called him in the last eight years? Had she sent him a postcard from God knows where? Maybe dropped by for Christmas dinner?

I didn't know. Suddenly it seemed wrong that I didn't know. I had known everything about him, once.

"Do you need a minute to look at the menu?"

I looked up and smiled at the server. "No, thanks. I know what I want." I glanced at Eli. "Are you ready to order?"

"I had plenty of time with the menu while you were out there on the sidewalk, thanks," he said drily.

I bit my tongue to keep from sticking it out at him. Eight years ago, I would have done just that. But things were different now. I didn't want to fall into our old playfulness. "I'll have the lamb burger, medium, with the yuca fries. And a glass of water with lemon slices."

The server nodded. "And you?"

"The same. But a Coke, no water."

"Great. I'll put these in and your food will be out soon."

And then we were alone again. Well, as alone as we could be in a restaurant full of people. Many of whom were sending curious glances our way. I almost couldn't blame them for being curious. Everyone knew our history and, anyway, when everyone knows everyone else, really good, *new* gossip is hard to come by. I pressed my lips together and lifted my chin. I wasn't about to give them anything to gossip about.

"We should probably get started." I dug into my bag and pulled out a notebook and pen. "I figured we should make a list of duties pertaining to the Fourth of July celebration and then divide them up."

"Sounds good."

I uncapped my pen with a flourish. "Item one, notify all the vendors that the Whittakers have left for California and that we will be handling matters from here on. Mayor Whittaker gave me the list and their contact information, so an email should do it."

"That sounds like the sort of official notice that should come from the mayor."

I nodded my agreement and wrote my name down in parenthesis next to item one. "Item two, the fireworks.

That would include permits and waivers of liability and so forth."

"I can do the logistics, but my guess is that it will be your official signature that's still needed."

I wrote his name down, followed by a slash and my own name. I frowned, staring at our names. Linked and yet separated. *Don't get sentimental, Emma.* I shook my head. "What else?"

"The pie-baking contest. Usually the mayor is one of the three judges. We need to make a change this year, because it can't be you."

I narrowed my eyes. "Why can't it be me? I like pie. This might be the only task of being mayor that I actually enjoy, and you want to take it away from me? I don't think so."

"For the past three years, I've been one of the judges. This year I turned down the honor because I intend to enter myself. Which means you can't be a judge either, seeing as you're biased as hell."

"I am *not* biased. When it comes to pie, I am completely impartial."

"You're biased when it comes to me. Think about it, Ms. Andrews." He leaned forward, elbows resting on the table, eyes locked onto mine. "Would you really let me win? Are you going to stand there in front of everyone and tell me my pie is the best thing you've ever tasted? Shake my hand? Pin that blue ribbon to my shirt?"

I stared at him. My mouth went dry and heat spread through me. It was ridiculous, absolutely ridiculous, that every word he said was punctuated by a bolt of lust. There was nothing sexual about shaking a man's hand or pinning a ribbon to his shirt. And yet the thought of doing that, of my palm touching his and his fingertips brushing the sensitive skin of my wrists, of feeling the muscles of his chest as I pinned the ribbon…it made me hot and achy. It was ridiculous. And unfair.

"Stop calling me Ms. Andrews," I said furiously. "It's weird."

"What should I call you, then?"

"You know my name."

He held my gaze for a moment before looking away. He leaned back in his seat, putting more distance between us. "It doesn't matter what I call you. You won't ever let me win."

He was right, though I hated to concede. Not because I was so biased that I couldn't recognize good pie when I tasted it, but because I knew if I were to shake his hand and touch his chest, I would burst into flames on the spot. My brain said *hell, no, not him*. My heart wailed about betrayal and broken friendship.

But my body? My traitorous body wanted him. I didn't know what to do with that. It was a brand-new experience, where Eli was concerned. Sure, back when we were friends, it might have crossed my mind once or twice that kissing him might be an interesting experience. But I had never let myself dwell on that kind of thought. Because we were friends, and friends didn't think about kissing. Or touching. Or how his hands looked like hands that knew how to *do things*.

"Two lamb burgers with yuca fries, a glass of water with lemon, and a Coke," the server said cheerfully, completely unaware of what he was interrupting. He set the food down. "I'll be back to check on you when you've had a minute to try everything."

"Thank you," we said in unison, both slightly subdued.

I shook out my napkin and spread it on my lap, glaring at Eli the entire time. Still glaring, I grabbed a fry, popped it into my mouth, and chewed. It was hard to stay angry with so much deliciousness happening in my mouth, but I managed it through sheer force of will.

After swallowing, I said, "Fine. I'll find someone else to replace me. Maybe Kate? She owns Sweet Things. You know, the candy store on Main Street by Nana's Yarn?"

"Sure..." His voice trailed off as his gaze drifted to something past my shoulder. His expression turned comically perplexed.

"What? What is it?"

"She's taking a picture of her food."

I shrugged. "Yeah. People do that. *I* do that, sometimes."

"Not like this."

I turned to see what he was talking about. It was hard to miss. There was a girl—early twenties, maybe?—standing on her chair, aiming her digital camera down at the table. Her friend had a ring light that appeared to plug into her phone, and a white board they appeared to be using as some sort of backdrop.

"Huh," I said. "Maybe Delmy is about to get a stellar review in *Food and Wine Magazine* or something." I turned my attention back to my food. "Anyway. What else do we need to do?"

"A walk-through of the fairgrounds wouldn't be a bad idea. Make sure we know where everyone is supposed to set up. What vendor goes where." He studied his burger like it was the most interesting thing in the world. "We should do that together."

Together. I choked on a mouthful of burger. "Is that really necessary?"

He raised an eyebrow. "The Fourth of July celebration is a huge deal. But if you want to ruin it for everyone, that's your call, I guess."

Damn him. "All right. Together."

Funny how the more I tried to stay away from him, the harder fate threw us together. But I didn't believe in fate. What I did believe in was this: Come July 5, the votes of Hart's Ridge would be tallied, and I would never speak to Eli Carter again.

Chapter 8

Eli

It was one o'clock, which meant that it was time to make my standard Wednesday afternoon rounds. I usually began at the south side of town, where the Donnelly family had been raising chickens for three generations, and made my way to the north side and the Christmas tree farm, with several stops along the way. Checking in with neighbors. Heading off disputes before they could become a crisis. That was what I *should* do.

Instead, I was rooted to the sidewalk, wondering what it was about seeing Emma swoop her pale hair off her neck and twist it into a tidy bun with smooth, efficient motions that made it difficult to breathe.

"Ugh," she muttered. "When will this heat wave end?"

"I hear temperatures might go down to the sixties," I said before I could stop myself. It was a mistake. We didn't joke with each other. We didn't tease. We weren't *friends*.

She spun around on her toes. "When?" she demanded.

I grinned. "October."

From her half-groan, half-laugh, she had forgotten, too. But not for long. I saw the instant she remembered. Her lips flattened and the light in her eyes turned cold.

"So," she said. "I'll see you Saturday. For the walk-through."

"Right. Saturday."

She gave a crisp nod and took a step toward her truck...and then stopped. Her head tilted. I watched, fascinated, as she slowly circled the lamp post.

"Dammit," she muttered, making the most adorably grumpy face I had ever seen.

"What?" I asked. I looked from Emma to the lamp post and back again. "What's happening?"

"The lamp post is in terrible shape, that's what's happening," she said, looking like it was a personal affront to her. "They're *all* in terrible shape."

I took a good, long look. She wasn't wrong. The paint was chipped and peeling pretty badly. I shrugged. "Yeah. I mean, they're what? A hundred years old? Of course they look bad."

"They would look better with a new coat of paint." She tilted her head back, shielding her eyes from the sun with her hand, as she studied the top of the pole. "See those curved hooks? It looks like they were meant to hold something. Maybe flower baskets? That would probably look nice." She was visibly annoyed by the idea. "Dammit!"

"What's wrong with flower baskets?" I wanted to know.

"Because now I have to figure out how I'm going to do that. So I can leave Hart's Ridge better than I found it."

My heart stopped. A physical impossibility, maybe, but it was the only way to explain the sudden halt of blood flow to my brain, making me light-headed. "You're leaving Hart's Ridge?"

"No." She frowned. "It's an expression. Leave it better than you found it. It's—" She turned away abruptly, leaving the sentence unfinished.

And then I remembered, with a flash of nostalgia that punched me in the gut. A picnic by the river that ran down Hart Mountain. How old were we then? Ten? Eleven? The empty beer cans littering the riverbank hadn't been ours, but Mrs. Andrews had insisted we pack them up anyway to throw in the garbage can at home. *Leave it better than you found it.*

"It's what your mom always told us," I said quietly.

"Yes."

I nodded. "Okay, then. So the lamp posts. Fixing them up, that will be your contribution as mayor? To leave it better than you found it?"

"Well, what else am I going to do? I can't stop the processing plant from closing. I can't do some math magic that fixes the deficit without raising taxes. I'm not..." She made a noise of frustration. "I'm not smart. Not the kind of smart a person should be, if a person is mayor. I got B's and a few C's from elementary school up through high school and failed out of community college. You know that."

"Stop it," I said sharply. I hated it when she put herself down like that. It didn't happen often. Emma was pretty confident in herself, for the most part. But this had always been a sore spot with her. She had never been a great student, despite the fact that both her parents were teachers.

In ninth grade, they had subjected her to all kinds of testing, trying to figure out what the problem was. Fuck, that was painful, watching her hope fade each time another test came back negative. No ADD, no ADHD, no dyslexia. No explanation at all. Generally speaking, I liked Emma's parents, but in those moments I had wanted to shake them. What was wrong with B's, anyway? Didn't they know how amazing she was?

"There are lots of different kinds of smart," I said now, and meant it. Emma was one of the smartest people I knew.

Her wry smile made my heart twist in my chest. "Ever noticed how people only say that to people like me? No one ever says that to straight-A students."

"You're smart."

"Not the right kind of smart, the kind who's a whiz with numbers. That's the kind of smart Hart's Ridge needs right now. I can't do that, but *this*, I can do. I can paint a lamp post." A look of doubt crossed her face. "I think so, anyway."

I didn't say anything to that. Not because I had any doubts in her ability to paint a lamp post. I didn't have a single one. I had known her since the first day of kindergarten, and not once had Emma Andrews had an idea that she failed to follow through on.

No, I stayed quiet because Emma always did her best thinking out loud, and I didn't want to miss a word of it.

"Cost isn't a problem, if I'm providing the free labor," she muttered, more to herself than me. "The town maintenance fund can cover a few gallons of paint."

She scratched a fingernail against the surface, chipping off little bits of paint, and frowned. "I'll have to sand off this old, rusted stuff first. Oh my God, that's going to suck. I wonder what kind of paint works on cast iron? I'll have to ask Noah at the hardware store. Or the internet. The internet knows everything."

I nodded in agreement, though I doubted she noticed. She was in her own world now, where I didn't exist. For once, that didn't bother me.

"Twenty lamp posts, seven feet tall... I think I have a ladder that could work...maybe. Hm." She stepped back, hands on her hips, and looked the lamp post up and down. "Boost me up."

I blinked. "Say that again?"

"Boost me up." She waved impatiently, motioning me closer. "The top of my ladder reaches about to your waist, maybe a little higher. I want to see if I can reach the top of the lamp post from there."

I wasn't about to protest. She was going to touch me, willingly, and I didn't care that the touching would only consist of being stepped on. She could walk all over me, if that was what she wanted to do.

I dutifully shifted my body between her and the lamp post, laced my hands together, and crouched down. "Okay, then. Come on."

She took hold of my shoulders for balance and stepped onto my waiting hands.

"Hang on tight," I said. "I'm going to stand. You ready?"

"I—" Her voice came out raspy. She cleared her throat. "Yes. I'm ready."

I tried not to let that bother me, that she was clearly nervous. "Don't be scared. I'm not going to drop you. Hold tight to me, okay?"

She didn't answer, but her fingers dug into my shoulders. I stood slowly, so damn slowly, her body sliding against mine as she moved with me. Fully straightened, her feet were braced at my waist, and my eyes were level with the waistband of her jeans.

"Oh," she said cheerfully. "This is good. This is perfect."

Perfect? I bit back a groan. It was *torture*. She smelled so good. So...edible. Literally edible. Like tortillas and peppers and spices. Nothing like anyone else. Claire had worn some kind of floral perfume that made me sneeze. Emma's scent didn't make me sneeze. It made me hungry. For burritos...and other things.

"I don't even have to stretch to reach the top." She lifted her arms.

I could tell she lifted her arms because her T-shirt came up, revealing a strip of soft, pale stomach and the most lickable belly button I had ever seen in my life. I didn't consider belly buttons lickable, as a rule, but hers was. I wanted to delve my tongue in that shallow indentation, swirl, and then move farther south. *Yes*.

No. The thought of putting my lips there, at the juncture of her thighs, made my mouth water and my insides weaken, and I couldn't afford to weaken with Emma literally depending on me to stay strong. I gritted my teeth.

"You almost done using me as a stepladder?" I asked, torn between hoping and dreading her answer was yes. I didn't want to stop holding her, but how much more could I take before I gave in to temptation and licked her navel?

"Right. Sorry." She gave me a soft pat on the head, like I was a dog or something. "You can put me down now. Wait. You know what? I'll just jump." Without waiting for my reply, she pushed off from my shoulders and hopped down. "Thanks."

"Yeah." I looked at the marks from her shoes crisscrossing my palms. It hadn't hurt, but then again, I hadn't really been paying attention to how my *hands* felt. I had been much more focused on the mere inch of air that had separated her skin from my mouth. "No problem."

She looked at me, then quickly looked away again like she was embarrassed. Her mouth opened and closed but no words came out. Finally, she shook her head, an answer to a question I hadn't yet asked.

"What?" I said.

She pushed back a lock of hair that had escaped the bun and tucked it behind her ear. "I keep forgetting I'm mad at you."

I stopped breathing. I took an unconscious step toward her, hoping. Longing.

It was the wrong move.

She backed up, keeping the distance between us. "But I *am* mad at you. I'll always be mad. It doesn't matter how nice you are, how familiar it feels to be near you, how—it doesn't matter. None of it. Nothing can change that you arrested my dad. He didn't even have a chance."

I let out the breath I had been holding, long and slow. "I know. It isn't fair. You're right to be mad."

She frowned, her eyebrows pushed together in a straight line. "Stop being reasonable about it. You can't make me change my mind. We can't be friends again."

"I'm not trying to change your mind." I knew better than that. No one ever changed their mind, not when it came to me. My mom had loved me—so she had said—but I hadn't been able to talk her into staying with me, either. Emma was no different. Forgiveness, unconditional love...that was for other people, if it existed at all. Not for me.

"No. No, I guess not." There was a note of resignation in her voice that I didn't understand. Wasn't this what she wanted?

I couldn't ask her, because she was already turning away, getting into her truck, slamming the door behind her with a finality that reverberated in my soul.

It wasn't lost on me that someone else was always doing the leaving.

I was the one left behind.

I was nearly at North Star Farm when I got the call.

"We got the Naloxone in," Chrissy Davis said. "You want to swing by the clinic and get it?"

"I'll be there in twenty," I said, already making the U-turn. *Finally.*

Eight years ago, I would have said that, outside of loose animals, the biggest part of my job was handling disturbances, usually due to meth, and usually ending in an arrest. Now, the biggest part of my job was still disturbances, usually due to opioids, possibly ending in a night at the Hart's Ridge Free Health Clinic, but usually recuperating at home. I had Chrissy to thank for that.

The Health Clinic was one of the best things that had happened to Hart's Ridge, but it came at a price. Hart's Ridge had to make a choice: It could expand the two-bed jail to thirty beds, with a corresponding increase in police officers, or it could build a health clinic. It couldn't afford both. Since the drug problem in Hart's Ridge was users, not dealers, the town chose the clinic. The right choice, in my opinion, but it meant that technically, the Hart's Ridge Police Department no longer existed. I was an officer for the Colby County Department, contracted to Hart's Ridge along with two part-time officers.

The change in employer hadn't changed my job much at all, though. Except I made fewer arrests. It turned out I was much less likely to arrest a person for a non-violent crime when I didn't have a place to keep them. Still a fuckton of animals on the loose, though. Abandoned dogs, cats in trees, cows on the run. Small town life.

Twenty minutes later I pulled into the parking lot. Chrissy was outside waiting with a big box and a clipboard.

"Hey, there," I said. "What have we got?"

"Twenty kits total. Fifteen of the nasal sprays, five of the injections." She gave me an apologetic look. "I know you said people are kind of squeamish about using the needles, but that was the best we could do."

"No worries. I'll take what I can get."

"Great. I'll need your signature here." She handed me the clipboard.

"Sure thing." I signed my name with a flourish, handed it back to her, and scooped up the box. "Thanks again, Chrissy."

She shook her head. "You don't have to thank me. You know we wouldn't be here without you."

"You would have found a way." I believed that. Chrissy put her heart and soul into the health center.

After dropping the box in the passenger seat, I gave her a wave. I couldn't stand around all afternoon talking when I had deliveries to make.

An hour later I was down seven kits. That was enough, for now. It would be six months before Chrissy ordered another box, so this would have to last.

I turned down Main Street for one last check. My shift was over, but that didn't mean much since I was almost always on call. I slowed down, noticing a half-dozen men had congregated outside the credit union. It was probably nothing—I recognized them as fairly staid community members—but I was curious, all the same. I pulled over and rolled down the window.

"What's going on?"

Mr. Elwood, the manager of the credit union, leaned down and peered in the window. "That's a good question, officer, and the truth is, we don't actually know."

"Sure, we do," another voice protested. "Emma Andrews has lost her mind, that's what's going on."

I was out of the car in a flash. "What do you mean?"

"See for yourself." Mr. Elwood jerked his head to indicate across the street. "She's scrubbing the damn lamp post. Been doing that all afternoon, in fact, starting at the south end of the street. Now, I wouldn't go so far as to say she's lost her mind, but it is peculiar."

I watched as Emma positioned the ladder and climbed up. Steadying herself with one hand braced on the post, she scrubbed hard with a wire brush. After a minute, she paused. Her head rolled in a tired circle and she rubbed the spot where her neck met her shoulder. Then she scrubbed some more.

"Is that what she thinks mayors do? Scrub lamp posts?" someone said, hooting with laughter. "Poor girl is in over her head."

I felt a rush of annoyance. "She's not just scrubbing them. She's sanding them. Getting them ready for painting. Then maybe hang some flower baskets. Make them look nice."

"Flower baskets, hey?" Mr. Elwood crossed his arms over his expansive stomach and rocked back on his heels, considering. "I like that. They haven't looked like that since I was a boy." Since Mr. Elwood was closing in on eighty, that would have been a good seventy years ago.

"Sure, you like it," said Jacob Bronson, who owned the only car dealership in town—among other businesses. "People like pretty things. But there's more to mayor than making a town pretty, and I don't see how Emma Andrews is up to the job. Hart's Ridge is in trouble. You think that little girl right there, scrubbing the damn lamp post, is going to get us out of it? No. One of us has to step up."

"One of us." Mr. Elwood snorted. "You mean *you*."

"No, I don't. You think I have time to be mayor? I have businesses to run. No, I mean this town's finest police officer, who just so happens to also be our newly appointed deputy mayor." Bronson clapped me on the shoulder. "I mean Eli Carter. He's our man."

Our man. I narrowed my eyes. I knew Bronson well enough to know that he meant those words literally. Bronson had no use for a police officer in his pocket, as he preferred to do his business legally, but he would love to have a mayor who owed him favors to make sure those legalities were smoothed away.

Unfortunately for Mr. Bronson, he was mistaken on two counts.

Number one, I couldn't be bought and paid for. I wasn't his man. I wasn't *anyone's* man.

Number two, this town needed a mayor with the creativity and tenacity to fix a problem that had sounded the death knell for other small towns throughout the entire country. This town needed a mayor who believed in leaving things better than she found them. This town needed a mayor who got off her ass and actually *did* something, even if it was only making lamp posts pretty again, while everyone else wasted time arguing about what *should* be done.

This town needed Emma Andrews.

The trouble was, Emma Andrews did not want to be mayor. So she said. Except there she was, painting streetlights. Because the streetlights were a problem, and she liked to fix problems. That was the truth about Emma, though she would likely never admit it: She *liked* to solve problems. And what was being mayor all about, if not solving problems? Damn shame she didn't think she wanted the job.

But then, Emma never wanted anything she didn't have to fight for.

What was it she had told me? *She didn't know what to do with herself when things were going right.* She needed things to go wrong. She needed an enemy to destroy. And in her mind, there was no bigger enemy than Eli Carter, the man who put her father in jail.

"What do you say, Eli?" Bronson asked. "You want to be mayor? Turn this town around?"

I tore my gaze from Emma. "I'm in."

Emma Andrews needed a fight, and I was going to give it to her.

Chapter 9

Emma

Everything hurt.

I groaned as I rolled out of bed, my muscles aching in protest. I had spent the better part of yesterday scrubbing the lamp posts with a wire brush and smoothing away the old paint. And I wasn't done yet. Ten down, ten more to go.

Despite the pain in my back and shoulders, I was up before the sun. I still had a business to run, one that couldn't be put on pause just because I now had the additional labor of being mayor. *Unpaid* labor. Fuck my life.

Today, though, would be different. Cesar and I couldn't stand around with nothing to do and no one to feed; we had bills to pay. If the customers weren't going to come to us, then we would go to the customers. Which was why we were driving an hour to the SuperMart a little ways past Asheville, where we would set up in the parking lot.

Cesar would be here any minute, so I hustled through my morning routine of brushing my teeth, throwing on clean but wrinkled clothes from the top of pile of laundry I hadn't had time to put away yet, and twisting my hair into a bun. I didn't have time to whip up an elaborate breakfast, and anyway Cesar was right. I couldn't really cook. Burritos were always an option, but not an appealing one since I would be making them all day and probably eat one for lunch.

I set a pot of coffee to brewing and sat down with a bowl of cereal just as Cesar walked in without knocking. He never knocked, not since seven years ago when he had knocked every day for a week, and every day for a week I had ignored him. He had finally let himself in without my permission, since the door was never locked anyway, and found me on the floor, staring at the fan.

Anyone else would have given up, but Cesar was my surrogate grandfather. His daughter, Helen, had been best friends with my mom growing up. It was a lifelong friendship, only ending when Mom died. Helen had tried to help me after Mom passed, but somehow it had been too painful for both of us. I couldn't be around Helen without wanting to break something, and she couldn't look at me without crying.

With Cesar it was different. I hadn't spent as much time with him as I had with Helen, so the memories associated with Mom were fewer. At the time, I needed fewer memories.

"I hitched up the Airstream to your truck." He helped himself to the coffee, filling his travel mug and adding a spoonful of sugar.

"Thanks."

My Yukon Denali was more than a decade old, but it could haul almost about anything. So long as I made wide turns and didn't push too hard on the gas, I mostly forgot the Airstream was there at all—until it was time to park. Luckily, that wouldn't be an issue where we were going. There would be plenty of space in the back of the parking lot.

Fifteen minutes later we were on the road, heading north. The sun was just rising, streaking the sky with pink and gold. My breath caught. I had seen thousands of sunrises exactly like it, but it hit me the same every time. The beauty of the Blue Ridge Mountains never got old.

The streetlights along the highway flicked off as the sky grew brighter. Streetlights were not something I had ever spent a lot of time considering, but now that I was so intimately acquainted with the lamps on Main Street, I noticed how ugly these were in comparison. Big and gray, with none of the delicate, intricate ironwork. None of the charm.

"Did you know that the streetlights on Main Street are a hundred years old?" I shared. "Noah at the hardware store told me. He said they were gas until about thirty years ago. Apparently the pipes were leaking, gas was getting under the ground and killing trees."

Cesar grunted. I took that to mean that, while he was not *per se* interested, it would be too much effort to shut me up.

"There's a company in Germany that makes replacements that convert gas to electric. They customize it so they use the same base mounting as the gas mounts. And then they use special light bulbs that mimic the tone of gaslight. Isn't that cool?"

Cesar grunted again.

"It was apparently a big deal at the time. Do you remember it?" I paused, giving him time to respond, but he just grunted again. "Hart's Ridge got a grant from the National Park Service. There's a Historic Preservation Fund that can pay for this sort of thing. I'm going to apply and see if I can get them to cover the buckets of paint I bought."

At the mention of money, Cesar perked up. "Get your labor covered, too."

I frowned. "That seems wrong, somehow. I'm mayor. I can't hire myself to do a job."

"Hart's Ridge isn't paying you for it. The Park Service is. You're not in a position to turn down money right now, especially not hard-earned money. You're doing the work, and I don't see anyone else who was stepping in. Get your labor covered."

"We'll see," I said noncommittally.

Cesar was right, I wasn't in a position to turn down money. My savings account could cover three months of expenses, barring emergencies, but when had I ever gone three months without an emergency? Getting paid for the hours she spent toiling on the streetlights would be a blessing. On the other hand, it might not be legal. The mayor didn't even get a salary. Maybe I couldn't be paid for odd jobs and services, either.

I sighed. It was only my second day as (acting) mayor, and I was already in over my head. How was I going to pull this off? It was like being tossed into a live video game and not knowing what the rules were.

Two months. That's all I had to do this for, was two months. If I did a good job, great. If I messed a few things up here and there, that would be fine too. City Council had set the special election for July 5. Whatever I screwed up between now and then, the new mayor would fix everything. I didn't know who that would be, but it didn't matter.

It wouldn't be me.

By the time we rolled back into town, I was exhausted down to my bones. There wasn't a single part of me that wasn't demoralized, from my greasy hair to my throbbing feet.

The day had been a success, if success meant earning a tidy profit that covered our expenses, including gas and wages, plus a little more. For the first time in a month, the tightness in my chest eased somewhat. I wasn't going to lose the house. Not yet, anyway. I could still pay Cesar's wages, which was a huge relief. So yes, the tightness in my chest had eased.

But everything else ached. What didn't ache physically ached existentially. Those were worst of all. I hated existential aches.

We had sold out at SuperMart. That was good. But it had taken us all day to do it, and that was bad. The sun had been rising when we left this morning, and now it was setting. Worse, we had spent *three hours* driving. What had been an easy hour-long commute this morning had turned into a two-hour slog through traffic on the return home.

Was this going to be my life? Burritos from sunup to sundown, and three hours in traffic? The thought of it made my stomach curdle with dread.

I wasn't opposed to hard work. The Airstream was open seven days a week and I worked all seven of them. It wasn't the same, though. For one thing, the Airstream closed at three, which meant I was done by four. That left plenty of time to get a happy hour drink with Kate and Suzie—which, more often than not these days, consisted of club soda for Suzie as she was either pregnant or nursing—or to binge a television show if I wanted. I might not always have time to fold laundry, but at least I had enough spare time and energy to make sure dust bunnies weren't rolling around and the dirty dishes didn't stack up.

For another thing, I didn't spend three hours driving. My commute was a five-minute walk from my front yard to the house, fifteen if I had to drive from the church or another location in Hart's Ridge. Sitting in a never-ending stream of cars full of irritated, aggressive drivers was soul crushing. Not to mention that gas wasn't exactly cheap for a Yukon.

Most importantly, I knew every single one of my customers in Hart's Ridge. I saw the same people day in and day out. Even the workers who commuted from outside Hart's Ridge. I knew their lives, their families, and how they liked their coffee. I liked hearing the gossip. I liked seeing familiar faces. Serving burritos from the Airstream meant more to me than just a paycheck.

Tomorrow we would be changing locations to Colby County Community College. It was fifteen minutes closer, and far enough from Asheville that we might avoid traffic. If school was in fall or spring session, a college campus would be a safe bet. We weren't sure how it would play out for the summer session. Maybe it would still be busy, who knew? It was a gamble, but I hoped it would pay off.

Right now, I was so tired I didn't want to think about it anymore. I didn't want to think about the streetlights, either, and how I was going to get them sanded and painted when all my daylight hours were devoted to burritos. I didn't want to think about how Kate and Suzie had probably had a great time at happy hour without me. I didn't want to think about why Eli's face was on a gigantic poster with *Vote for Law and Order* in big black letters.

Wait, what?

I hit the brakes and came to a stop there in the middle of Main Street, not bothering to pull over. I stared out the window, rubbed my eyes, then looked again. No, I wasn't hallucinating. *Vote for Law and Order*, then his serious, unsmiling face, followed by *Vote Eli Carter for Mayor*.

What. The. Hell.

"Oh, so we're doing this again," Suzie said, looking down at me. "Well, I'm not getting down there with you this time. I've gained a thousand pounds since yesterday, all in my stomach."

I kept my eyes on the ceiling fan's slow, lazy circles. "I didn't ask you to."

The floorboards vibrated beneath me as my friends plopped themselves down on the couch. "I take it she heard the news?" Kate asked.

"We saw the posters driving back into town," Cesar said. "She screamed a bit, and now here we are."

"Emma, honey, this isn't the end of the world," Kate cajoled. "Maybe it's even a good thing. You don't want to be mayor, right? Now you won't have to be. Obviously we hate him, so that's a factor to consider, but he might...maybe he would do a good job. And you would be off the hook. Wouldn't that be nice?"

"Theoretically, yes," I said.

But in reality? In reality it would suck.

I knew myself well enough to understand that I was not a practical, even-keeled sort of person. I didn't make decisions based on logic and reason. I was driven by emotion. Rationally, I knew that Eli was a decent human being who cared about Hart's Ridge, and our painful history didn't change that. As mayor, he wasn't going to go outlawing food trucks or raising taxes on small businesses. My life would continue on the same as it always was.

But *emotionally*. Emotionally, everything would change. Hart's Ridge wouldn't feel like home anymore. It would be *his* town. He would preside over all my favorite events, like the Christmas tree lighting and the Fourth of July fireworks. His infuriatingly handsome face would be *everywhere*.

It would be intolerable. Absolutely intolerable.

I would have to leave. This town was only big enough for the both of us when I could pretend he didn't exist. There would be no more pretending if Eli were mayor.

Leaving Hart's Ridge had never occurred to me. Then again, it had never occurred to me *not* to. Leaving had never been an option, not with my dad in the Asheville prison. I needed to stay close to him while he was there, and to be a soft place to land when he got out.

Every decision I had made had been focused on immediate survival, not the future or ambition. Had I *wanted* to run a food truck? Not particularly. But that was the opportunity that had presented itself when I needed a job. Fortunately, it turned out I enjoyed cooking—or at least I didn't hate it—but it wasn't my passion the way it was for Delmy Garcia, who put her heart and soul into Dreamer's Café.

What *was* my passion? I had no idea. What the hell did passion even matter, so long as bills got paid? Passion was a luxury, and quite frankly, I couldn't afford it.

Staying in Hart's Ridge, that was just happenstance, too. Dad would have sold the house if I had asked him to, but I couldn't have asked it of him. He needed something stable waiting for him when he got out. And I loved the house, truly. Anyway, I had flunked out of community college, so where would I go? What would I do for money? It wasn't like I had talent to fall back on, either.

No, I had never considered leaving, but I had never *chosen* to stay.

Now...now I was considering what it would be like to actually leave. And goddammit, I was staying. Hart's Ridge was *mine*. I loved it. Loved the mountains. Loved the people. Loved the buildings. Loved the freaking lamp posts I had sacrificed my muscles to scrub free of rust. Maybe I wasn't passionate about cooking burritos, but I was passionate about this. About Hart's Ridge.

I couldn't let Eli take it from me. I *wouldn't*.

But how was I going to stop him? Who was stupid enough to go up against Eli Carter, beloved officer of Hart's Ridge and all around hottie?

I was.

Lord help me.

"Emma." Suzie nudged me none too gently with a swollen foot. "You okay? You've been quiet for a really long time."

"Just thinking." The fan kept spinning, and I kept watching. It soothed me. Ordered my thoughts. "You know why small towns survive? The same reason big cities do. They either make something people want or they're a place people want to go. Like, L.A. makes movies and New York makes...I don't know, stocks or whatever."

"I don't think they *make* stocks," Kate murmured.

I ignored her. "And Piedmont, that's where all the good ski resorts are and the ritzy shopping, so people go there. Hart's Ridge made chicken parts."

"Gross." Suzie wrinkled her nose. "You're lucky I'm past the nauseous part of this pregnancy, because you're directly in my path."

"But it's true. That's what we did for the world. Now we don't. So how is Hart's Ridge going to survive? People have to come here. They have to spend money here. That's the only answer. I don't know why they don't. The scenery is gorgeous, the food is amazing—"

"Thanks," Cesar said.

"—and there's a ton to do here. Hiking and kayaking and all that. People *should* come here. They would love it. You know, some girl with two million followers on social media posted a picture of her lunch at Dreamer's Cafe yesterday, and today Delmy had more customers coming in from Asheville than she knows what to do with." I had stopped on our way back from SuperMart to pick up a quick dinner to go, and Delmy had told me all about it.

"If this were a movie, that's what the heroine would do, you know," I continued. "She'd turn her house into a bed and breakfast, like her parents had always wanted. She'd contact that girl with the two million followers and a few more like her and invite them to test it out before she opened. She'd set it up so that their visit coincided with the Fourth of July celebration. That would be smart. They would post pictures all over social media, and more people would come. It would all be a huge success, the town would have a new industry to see them through, and her enemy would rue the day he ran for mayor against her." I lifted a fist like I was making a vow. "Rue. The. Day."

For a moment no one said anything, and then Kate broke the silence. "Oh, my God," she whispered. "You're going to run for mayor."

The hair on the back of my neck stood on end as the epiphany hit me. "Yeah. I'm going to open a bed and breakfast, invite social media influencers, make this year's Fourth of July celebration the best one Hart's Ridge has ever seen, and Eli will rue the day he ran against me. Why not?"

Because it was insane, that's why not. But hell, in my experience, insane plans were the best kind.

Cesar cleared his throat. "Well, shit, girl. You thought of something."

Chapter 10

Eli

"Elias Robert Carter, you turn around and face me, you coward."

I couldn't stop the shit-eating grin from spreading across my face at her use of my full name. Lord, she was *pissed*. The fun kind of pissed. The kind where she was about to give me a good dressing down instead of ignoring me for another eight years. I wasn't stupid enough to say it to her face, but I had always...*enjoyed*...Emma's temper in a way I wasn't sure she would appreciate. It made my dick hard.

I turned slowly, careful not to slosh the coffees I was carrying. We had agreed to meet here, at the fairgrounds, at the ungodly hour of seven a.m., which meant coffee and pastries were required. "Good morning, ma'am," I said, schooling my features into wide-eyed innocence.

Her hands went to her hips and her expression turned thunderous. "Don't you *ma'am* me, Eli. I know what you did. What do you have to say for yourself?"

"I brought you coffee. And a donut."

Her gaze flicked to my hands, taking in the cardboard tray I balanced with one and the white paper bag I gripped in the other. Her expression softened just a little. "From Hot and Wired?" she asked hopefully.

"Of course." I pulled out a Boston cream for myself and handed her the bag. "I didn't know if you still liked lemon jelly."

I wasn't about to admit how long I had stood at the counter in Hot and Wired, contemplating the choices like it was life or death. Maybe Emma would have preferred an iced coffee, since it was supposed to get pretty hot today. Then again, it was still early enough that the fog hadn't burned off, and it was barely fifty-five degrees. I'd finally decided on hot coffee with skim milk, no sugar, which was how she drank it eight years ago. Had her tastes changed? I hated that I didn't know. What should have been a simple task was fraught with booby traps.

I didn't want to get this wrong. I had gotten so much wrong.

"I still like lemon jelly."

Thank God. My relief was short-lived, however, because she took a sip of her coffee and grimaced.

"What's wrong? You don't like the coffee?"

"It's fine," she said bravely. "It's...drinkable. What's in it?"

"Skim milk. Nothing else."

"Ah. You remembered what I used to like, way back when." Something flitted across her expression that I couldn't quite decipher. "I've become a better person since then. I take cream now, the heavier the better. Still no sugar, though. I prefer to save sweetness for pastries." To emphasize her point, she took a huge bite of donut and moaned. "Oh, my *God*. Amazing."

Another moment where she forgot she hated me. I basked in it. I took a sip of coffee, trying to hide the obscene pleasure I was taking in the way she demolished her donut.

"Don't think you can bribe me." Her donut half gone, she apparently remembered her anger. "I saw the posters. You're running for mayor."

"Sure am." I sipped my coffee and watched her cheeks pinken with anger. It was good coffee. Hot and Wired was the only coffee shop in Hart's Ridge, but I had never bemoaned the lack of a Starbucks or any of the other big chains that popped up on every city corner. "Is that a problem?"

It was clear from the way she was trying to incinerate me with her eyes that yes, it was a problem, as far as Emma was concerned. *Good*. Exactly what I had intended.

"You said you didn't want to be mayor. I thought we were on the same page."

"I changed my mind. Someone had to step up, and so far, we haven't had any takers. Maybe you've noticed? And, let me remind you, *you* didn't want the job either. So I'll ask you again. Do you have a problem with me running for mayor?"

She tore off a bite of her donut and glared at me while she chewed.

Suddenly I was angry. Angry that she wouldn't fucking *admit* it, already. She liked to pretend that I was nothing to her, that in her world I didn't exist. I had made that easy for her.

To hell with that.

I *existed*, dammit. It was time for us both to face the truth. I wasn't nothing. Not to her. Even if I was her enemy, that made me *something*. If I were mayor, she wouldn't be able to deny that.

Maybe...maybe I hadn't had the purest of intentions when I threw my name in the hat. Sure, I wanted what was best for Hart's Ridge, and that was Emma. And yeah, I wanted what was best for Emma, and that was Hart's Ridge. That's what I had told myself, and it was all true.

But maybe there was also a tiny, not-so-altruistic part of me that wanted to prove to her that I mattered to her, for better or worse. To make her see that she couldn't ignore me forever. If I were mayor, she could never ignore me again.

"You said you didn't want it for yourself, right?" I asked, trying to goad her out of her silent fuming. "So why not me?"

"Maybe I changed my mind," she muttered.

I leaned forward, cupping my ear. "What was that? I didn't quite catch it."

She glared mutinously. "You know damn well what I said, Eli. I changed my mind. I think I could do something good for this town, and I'm going to give it my all. You want to be mayor, Eli? You'll have to beat me first."

A slow grin spread across my face. "Well, then, Ms. Andrews, you've got yourself a fight. The acting mayor running against the acting deputy mayor. Won't that be fun?"

"Fun is not the word that comes to mind, no." Her eyes darted back and forth, and I could practically see the gears turning in her brain. "You can't be mayor unless you quit being a cop. Are you really going to do that?"

"Maybe I'll just get the law changed. Did you ever think of that? Have the City Council approve the salary instead of the mayor. Easy." I had no idea what changing a law actually entailed, and I had his doubts that the process was easy, but Emma didn't need to know that.

Realizing I was in imminent danger of having coffee thrown in my face, I abruptly turned and strode toward the long, red barn. "Keep up, Ms. Andrews. We have work to do."

I didn't look behind me, but I knew she was following by the angry stomping sounds.

"I told you to stop calling me Ms. Andrews," she said when she had finally caught up with me. "We played hopscotch together."

I ignored this. "Here is where we set up the food vendors last year. Inside the barn were picnic tables where everyone could sit and eat. The tables should still be there. Might need to clean them up some." I heaved open the heavy sliding doors. "Yep. Still here."

Emma followed me inside. "I forgot how big it was."

The only thing that stopped me from cracking a *that's what she said* joke was that the sight of her standing in the single shaft of sunlight damn near made me swallow my tongue. Everything was muted in the dim light, but not Emma. She gleamed like some untouchable goddess. I wanted to poke her in the arm, just to make sure she was human.

That was a good way to lose a finger, so instead I popped the last bite of donut into my mouth. "So, what do you think? Same setup as last year?"

There was a smudge of chocolate on my thumb. I sucked it off, not missing how her eyes glazed slightly as they tracked my movement. *Interesting.* Turnabout was fair play, even if that turnabout came eight years later. Back then, Emma had been the queen of mixed signals. The little touches. An innuendo here and there. I wasn't a jackass; I knew at least half of it was unintentional. Could she help it if licking an ice cream cone gave me ideas? But the other half...yeah, that had made me wonder. But I had always been too chicken to find out.

"What are you thinking?" I asked. "Same old setup or something different?"

"Oh. Right." She blinked several times, discomfited. A flush spread over her cheeks. I enjoyed that. "I was thinking...something different."

"Oh, yeah?"

"Yeah." She turned slowly on her toes, taking in the whole barn. "A band. Fairy lights. Dancing."

"What the hell are fairy lights?"

"This." She pulled out her phone, tapped a few words, and held it up for me to see the screen. "It would be beautiful, right?"

It would be. I could imagine it all. A warm July night, delicate strings of lights like dew on a spider web, Emma in a sundress that showed plenty of skin.

Stupid. Emma didn't wear dresses.

That was fine, because the image in my mind changed to Emma in a pair of jeans that molded to her gorgeous ass like second skin. I could live with that. More than live with that. I could—*shit*.

It was annoying how spending time with Emma left me constantly on the verge of being uncomfortably hard.

"What do you think?" she asked, completely unaware that a truthful answer to that question would make her run screaming from the barn. Or kick me in the nuts. It could go either way.

"I think—" My voice was rough. I cleared my throat and tried again. "I think that's a good idea. Do you have a band in mind?" She was still carrying the paper bag from our donuts, now empty, I realized. I took it from her, crumpled it into a small ball, and shoved it into the pocket of my jeans. Hopefully she didn't notice that I used the opportunity to create more space in the crotch region.

"Well, I only thought of the whole dance idea two minutes ago, so no. I mean, there are a few local to Asheville that are pretty good. Maybe the Lady Killers? It depends on who's available."

"Right."

She took another look around the barn and then nodded. "I think we're done here. Let's walk around the rest of the property."

I gestured for her to go first. "After you, Ms. Andrews."

Chapter 11

Emma

I gritted my teeth so hard my jaw ached. Swear to God, if he called me Ms. Andrews one more time, I would...I would...Well, I would do something terrible, to be determined later.

Why was he so goddamn polite all the time? With his *Ms. Andrews* and his *ma'am* and bringing me coffee and a donut? It made me feel feral. I wanted to scream and yell, muss up his hair, wrestle him to the ground until his ironed clothes were every bit as wrinkled as mine, bring him down to my level. He had no right to be so kind to me. Why couldn't he make it easy to hate him? Why did he have to be so damn perfect? It was infuriating.

I followed him out of the darkness and into the sunlight, squinting until my eyes adjusted. He slid the door closed behind us, the roped muscles of his forearm tensing under the strain, and a bolt of lust sent my insides quivering in response. *No. No, no, no.* How dare my body betray me like this? It was worse than infuriating. It was repulsive that my body refused to be repulsed by him.

Before I could stop myself, I reached out, brushing the length of his forearm with my fingertips. He froze.

"Sorry." A lie. I wasn't sorry at all. "I thought I saw a spider." There was no spider.

My fingers tingled. I could still feel the warmth of his skin, the soft tickle of hair. Touching him had been a mistake. I clenched my hands into fists so I wouldn't repeat it.

He still hadn't moved, hadn't said a word. It was beginning to scare me.

"Eli..." I hesitated, not knowing where to go from there.

"Tell me why you don't want me to be mayor," he said, his voice low.

"You know why."

"I want you to say it." He moved toward me, a determined glint in his eyes.

I took a step back, expecting he would take the hint and give me space. Like he always did. When he didn't, I took another step back, and another. My spine hit the wall of the barn, leaving me nowhere to go. He crowded into my space, braced one arm against the wall next to my head, and leaned in.

"Say it."

I raised my chin, meeting his gaze squarely, ignoring the sudden heat in my belly. "No."

For some reason, this seemed to amuse him. The corners of his mouth tilted up, and the fire in his eyes licked hotter. "What's the matter, Ms. Andrews?" His voice was a low, seductive growl. "Chicken?"

Ms. Andrews. Again! The absolute *nerve* of this man. Fury and lust swirled into a tornado inside me until I couldn't tell which was which. I grabbed his face with both hands, bringing him even closer. The stubble of his unshaved jaw scraped against my palms and I dug my nails against his skin in retaliation, enough to leave temporary marks, but not draw blood.

"Because I can't stand to look at your face every damn day, that's why. Is that what you want to hear? Because when I look at your face, I want to kick you or kiss you, and I don't ever seem to know which urge will win. Do you have any idea what that's like?" I demanded.

His gaze burned into mine. "Yeah. I know what that's like."

My heart was pounding so hard I was sure he could feel the vibrations. What the hell was happening to me? I knew lust. I knew hate. But having them mingled into a unified storm entirely focused on Eli Carter was something that genuinely shook me to my core. I couldn't begin to process it. All I could think was that his mouth was inches from mine, and maybe someone should do something about it.

And then he did.

He dipped his head and his lips crashed against mine.

Eight years ago, ten years ago, twelve years ago…I had, on occasion, allowed myself to imagine what it would be like if Eli kissed me. Sweet. Gentle. Maybe a little shy. A tentative question of a kiss.

This was nothing—*nothing*—like I had imagined all those years ago. It wasn't gentle. It wasn't sweet. There was no question to be answered here, only demands with which I eagerly complied. It was a struck match hitting gasoline and the explosion was instantaneous. We didn't ease our way into it. The kiss burned out of control from the moment of first contact.

I released his face only so I could get a better grip on him by digging my fingers into his thick, dark hair. I angled my head, parting his lips with my own before sliding my tongue into his mouth. He groaned, a rough, fierce sound unlike anything I had ever heard from him. He had always been so gentle with me. So careful.

He wasn't careful now. And, God, I couldn't get enough of it. Finally, *finally*, he was on my level, down in the mud with all the rage and need and things I couldn't say out loud.

He put one hand on my hip, gripping me hard enough that pain mingled with pleasure, holding me still so he could press his hard body against me. I knew I could tell him to stop, that it was enough now, and he would. But it wasn't enough. I wasn't sure it ever would be. How could I ever get enough of this? Enough of *him*?

Pleasure rocked through me, and I arched my hips, grinding shamelessly against him. The scrape of his shirt buttons against my chest tightened my nipples into hard points. I could feel the hard ridge of his arousal between my legs, sending a shock wave of need straight down to my core. No, I could never get enough of this. Of him.

He shifted, breaking some of the contact, and I growled—a sound so feral I was shocked it came from me—and dragged him back to my mouth.

Suddenly everything changed. The hand on my hip gentled, the ferocious press of his lips turned sweet.

"Emma-bear," he whispered, before lightly nipping my earlobe with his teeth.

The sudden onslaught of emotion slapped me in the face like a stinging wind, making my eyes smart. Oh, hell no. I was not going to cry. I was *not*. This wasn't rage or lust or even the storm of them combined. This was so much worse than that. It was…it was…Well, it didn't matter what it was. It was bad. I could take whatever heat he brought and more, but the tenderness… Oh, God. The tenderness nearly undid me.

My heart squeezed tight, and suddenly I was letting go, pulling back, pushing him away. It didn't take much. He went easily. So damn easily. I tried not to let that hurt too much. After all, I had been the one to tell him to go. Always, it had been me.

But he never argued.

I was shaking. My hands that had held him close, my knees that had still not recovered from that first explosive touch, and everywhere in between. Was I shaking because we had kissed, or because we had stopped? I honestly didn't know. Both, probably.

"We should take a look at where the Ferris wheel will go," he said, like nothing had happened. "I had an idea that if we move it to the other side of the field, to the west of the barn instead of the east, people might get a good view of the sunset over Hart Mountain while they're up there."

Calm. Cool. Polite.

Just like always.

Damn him.

"Right," I said. "Right. Good idea. The whole site is pretty flat, but we should check out where you want to move it. See if there's anything that might cause a problem."

Like kissing. Maybe I would feel as compelled to kiss him there as I had against the barn wall. Kissing was definitely a problem.

"Eli, that can't happen again," I blurted out. "The kiss. It can't happen again. Just so we're clear on that."

"Yeah, I know." He sounded so weary. So...beaten. "It won't."

"You shouldn't have kissed me."

He came to a standstill, his hands clenching into fists before he relaxed them and rounded on me. "Don't make me say it."

I blinked, startled. "Say what?"

"This might be an asshole thing to say. A nice guy would let it go. But I'm not *nice*. I'm a good man, but I'm not nice. And the truth is you wanted that kiss. You just don't want to be responsible for it. Don't blame me for something that we did together."

Shame lashed at me. I had grabbed him by the *face*. What, exactly, had I thought he would do about it? Boop me on the nose? "You know...you know how I feel about you."

He shook his head, started walking again. "Honey, I don't think even *you* know you feel about me."

The truth of that statement left me breathless. I couldn't speak for fear I would scream.

But he wasn't done.

"You're right, though. It was a mistake for me to kiss you. It won't happen again. Because next time, *you're* going to kiss *me*."

Chapter 12

Eli

I had always wondered what would have happened if I had actually grown a pair and kissed Emma Andrews all those years ago. In my teenager mind, it would go one of two ways. Maybe she would have immediately pulled back, with some line or other about how we were better off friends.

Or maybe she would have kissed me back and we would have been happy for a few months before everything went to hell and I was left without even her friendship. Even if everything had gone right, even if I hadn't arrested her dad, it wouldn't have lasted with us. High school sweethearts didn't exactly have an outstanding record for longevity.

Not even in a small town like Hart's Ridge, where there weren't a whole lot of dating options.

Even before the shit with her dad, before either of us could imagine what the future held, I had suspected things between us couldn't end well if I kissed her.

Now I knew for sure, because I had kissed her and it had not ended well.

To say the least.

But *before* the ending, in those explosive moments between the first crash of our lips to when she pushed me away...*Christ*. Good didn't begin to describe it. I didn't have words for what that was. It was so far outside my realm of experience, I genuinely didn't know what to make of it. Sure, I had felt lust before. I had felt anger. But I had never felt them at the same time and so thoroughly consumed with one person. The combination was a potent blend that had made me somehow both forceful and needy.

That wasn't me. I wasn't forceful with women. I wasn't needy with sex. I didn't give angry kisses that left my own lips tender for hours after—God only knew what I had done to hers.

And now I was hard again just thinking about it. There was something wrong with me. There had to be. I had spent the last three days since our kiss in a near constant state of arousal and fury, and the only thing keeping me from hunting her down to finish what we'd started was my promise to her.

I wouldn't kiss her again. She would have to kiss me.

She would do it, too. Maybe it would take days, weeks—oh, good Lord, please don't let it be weeks, I would never survive that and my dick would fall off from depression—but she would come to me eventually. Oh, yes, she would. She had changed somewhat in the last eight years. She took her coffee with cream instead of skim, and her laugh came slower than it once had. But *this* had held true: Emma Andrews never left a job unfinished.

And I was very much unfinished. Painfully so.

Which was why I was standing on Main Street, watching Emma paint the last of the streetlights, my pants too tight across the crotch and my mind full of impure thoughts. I wanted her to paint my pole with her tongue.

Yes, there was definitely something wrong with me.

"Just what the heck is wrong with you, Eli?" a strangely familiar voice demanded, echoing my thoughts.

I turned around. "Suzie!" I grinned, genuinely happy to see her.

Suzie was close with Emma, but once upon a time she had been my friend, too. Along with Luke, we had spent our high school years as a tightknit foursome. And then I had arrested Emma's dad, and the battle lines were drawn right down the middle, boys against girls. That had hurt, even though I wouldn't have taken Suzie from Emma, not for the world. But still. I had always liked her. I hadn't realized how much I had missed her until now.

"How are you doing? When is this one coming?" I asked with a nod at her stomach.

Her eyes lit up and she gave her belly a fond rub. "Any day now. A girl."

"Yeah? Is Michael going to make it back in time?" Michael was Suzie's older brother. He had been, from what I knew of him, a fairly stable, reliable type, until last year when his wife had suddenly filed for divorce. Two days later, he took off for Kilimanjaro.

"No, he's in Switzerland now. He can't miss the summer climbing season. But he's talking about coming home for Christmas, so—" She broke off with a frown. "But I don't want to talk about Michael. You distracted me!"

"Sorry." I gave her a sheepish grin. "I was just so happy you were talking to me again."

"Don't you try to charm me with those long eyelashes, Eli. I'm not talking to you again. I'm *lecturing* you. There's a difference."

I sighed, having a pretty good idea of what the lecture would entail. *Emma*. "Any chance you want to continue the lecture over coffee?"

"No coffee for me, thank you. But I'll accept a treat from Sweet Things. They have these great lemon candies that I like to suck on. It makes the baby kick."

"Sure."

"You're paying."

"Of course."

I held the door for her and then followed her in. It was like stepping into Willy Wonka's Chocolate Factory, without the creepy factor. Everything was bright and cheerful, from the pink-and-yellow striped curtains to the jars of colorful candies.

I looked around curiously. I hadn't been here since the grand opening six years ago. Not because I didn't like candy, but because it had been pretty clear from the way Emma had hugged Kate Gonzales, the owner, that they were good friends, which made this place her domain.

Which meant—

Shit. It was an ambush. I gave Suzie a reproachful look when Kate popped up from behind the counter like a jack-in-the-box.

"Officer Carter." Kate's eyes narrowed. "I wasn't expecting you so soon. Suzie, I have those lemon drops for you."

"Yay, candy." Suzie reached into the pink-and-yellow striped paper bag Kate offered her and popped one into her mouth. "I found him on the sidewalk, stalking Emma like a total perv."

"Hey!" I protested. "I wasn't—" I paused, remembering what my thoughts had been. Definitely a little pervy. "I wasn't *stalking* her. I just happened to be patrolling the street at the same time she was painting the lights. You know, doing my job?"

Kate's head tilted while she studied me. "Does your job also include making our friend angry every time she sees you?"

"Emma is always a little angry. That's part of her charm."

"She's been stomping around town for three days now, bossing the life out of everybody," Suzie said. "It's annoying."

"Three days, huh?" It had been three days since I kissed her, and apparently she was feeling the effects of that just as much as I was. I tried not to look too pleased about that. "Well, ladies, I'm real sorry about that, truly I am, but there's nothing I can do about it." Not until she let me, anyway. "So unless there's something else I can do for you—"

"There is," Suzie interrupted. She exchanged a look with Kate, who nodded. "You can drop out of the race."

I should have seen that coming, much like the entire ambush. But I had forgotten how devious Suzie Barnett could be, and how much she loved running people's lives for them. *Helping*, she called it. I always heard "helping" in quotation marks.

"Now, why would I do that?" I asked.

"Because if you win, Emma will leave. And we don't...that can't happen. We love her. And she loves Hart's Ridge. This is her home. She's been through enough, with her mom and her dad. Just let her be happy, already."

My chest felt like someone had placed a fifty-pound brick on it. Would she really leave Hart's Ridge if I won?

Yes.

I knew that in my bones. She had as good as told me that herself, right before I kissed her. And that was what I had wanted, wasn't it? Not for her to leave, but for her to care. For her to admit that I wasn't nothing to her, because hate, at least, was something.

Funny how it hurt just the same.

I had only ever wanted her to be happy...and safe.

But Emma leaving Hart's Ridge? Over my dead body. Fuck that.

"Then I guess you better make sure I don't win," I said.

Chapter 13

Emma

The last three days had been the busiest of my life. My mind was made up. I had to defeat Eli in the race for mayor. And since defeating Eli meant proving to the people of Hart's Ridge that I was the best mayor they ever had, I threw myself into the work heart, body, and soul.

Mostly body, actually. Who knew being mayor was such a physical job? My arms and shoulders still ached from scrubbing and painting the streetlights. Now in addition to that, my feet ached from walking up and down Main Street, talking to the owners of each and every business along the way.

Cesar had taken full responsibility for the food truck, roping in his grandson, who was a few years younger than me, to help. We were doing little better than breaking even there, but it was hard work now that we no longer had an easy setup. But that would change once I got the bed and breakfast up and running.

Maybe if I kept telling myself that, it would come true.

The first thing I had done after leaving Eli Saturday morning was submit my paperwork to City Council to get on the ballot. Well, no. The *very* first thing I had done was fume and cry to Suzie and Kate about how unfair Eli was, although I neglected to mention the kiss. *Then* I submitted my paperwork. From there, I hit the ground running.

And it was a *lot* of running.

If Hart's Ridge was going to get tourist money, those tourists were going to need a place to stay—something slightly classier than Goat's Tavern, which was, no offense to Luke, only a step or two above a tent. And that meant turning my home into the bed and breakfast of my parents' dreams.

It was surprisingly fun, picking out new furnishings for the guest bedrooms. Cost was a factor, but I had savings. So long as my plan worked, I could recoup the cost with future customers. Of course, if it didn't work, I'd be screwed. And broke.

And Dad—

And Hart's Ridge—

I gritted my teeth. *No*. I didn't have time for a doom spiral today. Everything was a risk, sure. Success wasn't guaranteed. But failure *was* guaranteed if I did nothing. Not just for me, but for Hart's Ridge. For Dad.

We were all in this together. There was no other way. With that in mind, I headed for Goat's Tavern.

The moment I crossed the threshold, nostalgia made my insides ache. Years ago, when we were kids and this was nothing more than a ramshackle barn, we all used to hang out here for long stretches of lazy hours—Eli, Luke, Suzie, and me. Luke's grandparents had retired from farming and his parents were off climbing mountains, leaving him to use the land how he wanted. It looked so different now and somehow still familiar. Luke had done a lot of work to turn it into a tavern, but the bones remained the same.

Actually, we had left our mark on one of these walls. It must still be here, somewhere. It was hard to get a sense of where, exactly, because Luke's decorating taste seemed to be "more is more."

The tavern was decorated for the holidays—all of them. Christmas lights were strung up behind the bar. Some of the tables had Halloween-type centerpieces, and some had Easter bunnies and eggs. Patriotic bunting in red, white, and blue lined one wall. It was...a lot. But somehow it worked. The whole place looked cozy and festive.

"Emma Andrews, it's about time you came to see me! Get your tiny ass over here and give me a hug."

I laughed. I wasn't tiny, but compared to Luke, everyone was. At six-three, he looked like he had just stepped out of a lumberjack catalogue, if there was such a thing. There ought to be, because most women and some men would pay good money to see Luke Buchanan, flannel sleeves rolled up to his elbows, chopping wood. Or whatever it was lumberjacks did.

I let him lift me off my feet in a big hug. "It's good to see you again."

"How are you, Emma?" He set me down on my feet again, smiling. "Let me tell Ethan to take over the bar, and we can catch up."

"Actually, I'm here on business."

His smile cooled. He crossed his arms over his chest. "Right. Okay. What can I do for you, Acting Mayor Andrews?"

Guilt hit me hard. Sure, I was here on business, but there wasn't anything wrong with catching up first, was there? We had been friends once, great friends. It wasn't his fault we didn't talk anymore.

No, that was on me. He had never taken sides. I was the one who refused to see him again after my dad went to jail, because I was afraid of running into Eli. And now I had gone and hurt his feelings. He deserved better than that.

"We can talk business later." Impulsively, I reached out and squeezed his arm—or tried to, anyway. It was like squeezing a tree trunk. "Let's catch up first."

"Awesome. I'll tell Ethan. What are you drinking? You want something to eat?"

"Vodka soda, light on the vodka because I'm driving. I already ate dinner, but I'll take some sweet potato fries. I've heard they rival Delmy's yuca fries." I considered myself a connoisseur of fries, and I wasn't about to pass up the opportunity to sample Luke's, no matter how full I was.

"You heard correctly. Grab that table in the corner and I'll join you in a minute."

"Great." I took a step and then paused, looking around, and called after him, "Hey, Luke, where's—"

"Under the dartboard." He grinned at my surprised face. "You're asking about our initials, right? I wanted them protected. You'll notice that there have been a lot of initials, and some profanities, added to these walls since then. So, under the dartboard, where the filthy animals couldn't get to it."

Hearing evidence that underneath the mountain man exterior still beat the most sentimental heart this side of the Mississippi made my chest tighten. Why had I stayed away for so long?

Because you're a terrible friend, that's why, came the accusing voice of my conscience.

I could fix that. I would just…add it to the list of everything else I needed to get done. I only had five minutes to contemplate how, exactly, I would do that when Luke returned with my vodka soda and a beer for himself.

"Fries will be out momentarily," he said, sliding onto the seat across from me.

"Great." I raised my drink and gave an appreciative nod. "Thanks."

He took a swallow of beer, then leaned back in his seat with a smile. "So, Madam Mayor. How did *that* happen?"

I groaned loudly, dropping my face in my hands. "Can you believe it? Me, mayor. It's ridiculous, isn't it?"

"I don't know. Asking me to be mayor and Ethan to be deputy mayor, now that was ridiculous. He hates people, especially if they want something from him. But you? You have a way of making things happen. You always have."

"What about you? You made *this* happen." I gestured to the room around me. "This place is amazing."

"Yeah, I'm pretty happy with it."

"Who is Goat? Did you pick up a new nickname since I last saw you?"

He shook his head with a laugh. "No. Goat is Goat. I'll introduce you before you leave."

"Sweet potato fries."

I looked up at the sound of a familiar voice to see Luke's younger brother balancing a platter of food. "Hi, Ethan."

He set the platter down in front of me. The spicy-sweet smell made my mouth water. "I thought he must be lying when he said you were here. I had to see it for myself."

I cringed inwardly at the unspoken accusation. Another innocent casualty in the war between me and Eli. Ethan was younger than Luke by eight years and had worshipped his older brother and his friends. "Well, here I am."

"Yeah."

He didn't say anything else, just stalked back to the bar. I bit my lip, watching him go. How many people had I hurt when I cut Eli from my life?

"Don't mind Ethan," Luke said. "That's just his way of saying don't stay away so long next time."

"There won't be a next time. Promise."

He reached forward, gave my hand a squeeze. "Good."

"Well, this sure looks cozy. I'm not interrupting anything, am I?"

I looked up to see Eli, arms crossed over his chest, mouth pressed into a firm line, dark eyes glittering. Even without his uniform on, power and authority rolled off him in waves. I snatched my hand back like I had been caught raiding the cookie jar before dinner.

"Hey, man. I was hoping you would swing by tonight," Luke said. If he noticed the air had suddenly gone thick with tension, he didn't show it. He cocked his head in my direction. "You should have brought Suzie along. We could have made it a reunion."

Eli continued to glower. "I didn't expect to see you here. It doesn't seem like your kind of place."

I narrowed my eyes. "And what kind of place would that be?"

"Wherever I'm not, would be my guess. You know I come here. You know my *friends* come here. Which means this isn't your kind of place."

The tension rolling off him gave me pause. Was he seriously mad that I had encroached on his turf? What did he think, exactly? That I was here to turn Luke against him? *Rude.* Okay, yes, once upon a time, I had done exactly that—with Suzie, not Luke. But that was when the wound was still fresh and I was still young. I wouldn't do that *now*. I might want nothing to do with Eli, but I wouldn't dictate who other people could be friends with.

Huh. Maybe I had grown up a little in those eight years. Who would have thought.

"I like it here," I snapped back. "I like Luke."

Luke beamed. "Of course you do, honey."

Eli clenched his jaw so tightly I could see the muscle tic in his cheek. "Outside. Now," he ordered through gritted teeth.

I stared at him with patent disbelief. "You must be joking. In the first place, because you do not get to order me around like I'm your lapdog. I am your boss now, thank you very much. Secondly, my fries would get cold, and cold fries are disgusting. And lastly, nothing good can come of me following you into the dark where there are no witnesses."

He raised an eyebrow. "Are you chicken, Ms. Andrews?"

It was exactly what he had said three days ago, right before I grabbed him by the face. Right before the kiss. Was it rage or lust that made my cheeks heat from the memory? A combination of both, probably. That seemed to be the way of things when Eli was around.

"Your schoolyard taunts have no effect on me. I am an adult." But because this was so obviously a lie—schoolyard taunts *always* got a rise out of me—I slid from my seat and stood. "Fine. We'll talk outside. Don't go anywhere, Luke. I'll be back in five minutes."

"It will take longer than that," Eli said. "You might as well go back to the bar."

I spun furiously to face him. "I am here to discuss business. Don't get in my way, Eli."

I pivoted on my toes and stalked toward the door. Out of the corner of my eye, I caught sight of the dartboard. I hated to ruin my dramatic exit, but I couldn't resist taking a quick peek. I lifted the dartboard and peered underneath.

There they were, four sets of initials, carved into the wooden beams. Suzie had encircled them with a heart because Suzie was like that. I slid the dartboard back in place with a hollow feeling in my stomach.

Funny how the marker of our friendships had outlasted the friendships themselves.

Chapter 14

Eli

I knew what Emma was looking for when she lifted the dartboard, but I didn't know if she would find it. I hadn't seen it for myself in five years, when Luke hung the damn thing after it became apparent that hikers liked to leave their own marks. For all I knew, five years of dart games had worn our initials smooth. Or maybe the wall was so scratched and scuffed that our initials weren't readable.

It was hard to tell by her subdued reaction. She didn't smile, didn't frown. It was a strange response for Emma. Her emotions were always close to the surface. Fury, ecstasy, despair, whatever she was feeling was usually written all over her face. But now her expression was carefully blank. It was unlike her, and it made me nervous.

She pushed open the door, leaving her palm against the rough wood just long enough to keep it from slamming shut in my face. I grinned to myself as I followed her into the warm darkness. Even pissed as hell, Emma couldn't bring herself to be rude.

The second the door closed behind us, she whirled to face me. "Well?" she demanded. "You have five minutes, Eli. My fries are getting cold."

"You—"

I broke off, nodding a polite hello to a twenty-ish man who looked like he hadn't seen a brush or razor in a month. Which he probably hadn't. Thru-hikers weren't known for their stellar hygiene. Then I grabbed Emma by the elbow and steered her around the corner, out of the yellow circle cast by the cast-iron lamps guarding the doorway. Random hikers might not care who we were, but plenty of nosy locals would be thrilled to have something to gossip about.

"Why are you here, Emma?" I asked, crossing my arms over my chest.

"Business, like I already told you."

I furrowed my brow. "Business? I'm the deputy mayor. I know it's weird because we're running against each other, but I should still know what's going on."

"It's not mayor business. It's *my* business."

"You mean the food truck?"

"No, I mean—" She paused, cocking her head to the side so her hair spilled over her shoulder, gleaming like a moonbeam. "I guess I didn't tell you. I'm turning the house into a bed and breakfast. I had this idea, that if people aren't coming to Hart's Ridge for work anymore, well, then maybe I could get them to come here for fun. And while they're here, they would need a place to stay, so I might as well get paid, too. The house would be a source of income instead of another bill I have to pay. Plus it would give Dad something to do when he gets home."

Interesting.

"Okay," I said slowly. "I'm all for people coming to Hart's Ridge for a good time and staying at your B and B. But how are you going to get them here? We don't have a resort like Piedmont. I mean, we have the same exact mountains as them, but no one even knows we're here. What's the plan, Emma? Because I know you have one."

She lit up like the finale Fourth of July fireworks. Christ, she was beautiful when she was excited about something.

"That's the best part. Have you noticed how busy Dreamer's is lately? Demy says it was all because of that girl who was here from L.A. We saw her taking pictures of her food, remember? Anyway, she has, like, two million followers on social media. She posted a picture of Demy's food, and suddenly everyone within an hour's drive of here showed up. I was thinking I could invite her back for the Fourth of July celebration, give her a free stay at the B and B, invite a few others like her, and *boom*. Business for Hart's Ridge. I mean, I hope so, anyway. What do you think?"

The question hit my bloodstream like a double shot of whiskey, making me feel a little unsteady on my feet. She cared what I thought?

"I think it's worth a shot. It could work. Yeah." It would take a lot of work, for sure, but Emma had never shirked from hard work—witness her determination in tackling the streetlights on Main Street. And I would help her, if she let me.

But maybe she had someone else in mind. *Luke*. Was that why she was here tonight? The question twisted my gut. Because I knew what kind of help most women sought from Luke. "So what does all this have to do with Luke?"

Her light dimmed slightly at the question. She crossed her arms, mimicking my posture. "You don't need to get all proprietary about Luke. I'm not going to take him from you. I know what I said eight years ago, but I'm not twenty anymore. He can be friends with both of us."

"I'm not being proprietary about Luke. I'm being proprietary about *you*." I leaned in, close enough that she could see the seriousness of my expression. I wasn't playing around here. This wasn't a game to me, and I wanted her to know that. "I don't want you here because I don't want you flirting with him. I don't want him touching you."

I watched her blink in confusion as she tried to make sense of my words. "I can flirt with whoever I want. But...I wasn't flirting. We were always just friends."

"You were just friends *then*. Now, he looks like he does and he knows it. I'm pretty sure there's a note about him in all the Appalachian Trail guides. *Stop by Goat's Tavern in Hart's Ridge. Have a beer and bang the owner.*"

Emma snorted with laughter. "Okay," she admitted. "Maybe I've heard a rumor here and there. Luke is certainly, um, *popular* with women. But that doesn't mean—" She broke off, frowning. "What's that noise? Is that...do I hear a goat?"

A goat? Oh, shit. I turned so fast I nearly gave myself whiplash, my eyes straining to see in the inky darkness. "Where? I don't hear anything."

"Huh." We were both silent, listening. "Maybe I imagined it?" she said uncertainly.

"Maybe." But I wasn't about to let my guard down just yet. The little bastard could be anywhere.

And then I heard it: the unmistakable crunch of a hoof on gravel. Slowly at first, one deliberate step after another, and then suddenly picking up speed as the beast broke into a run. I searched frantically through the darkness as the sound came closer. *There*. A few yards behind Emma, head lowered to better make use of its horns.

"What in the world—ahhhhh!" Emma ended on a shriek as I scooped her up in my arms.

"Not today, Satan!" I hollered.

Goat apparently disagreed. He rammed me behind my knees, sweeping my legs out from under me. With Emma still in my arms, I rolled mid-air, ensuring that I hit the ground with my shoulder, rather than my back or, God forbid, Emma.

By some miracle we fell onto the patch of soft grass rather than the gravel. She landed half on top of me, her head cradled by my bicep—because no way in hell was I going to let her head hit the ground—and her legs thrown over my thigh.

"What. The. *Hell*," she gasped out. "What was that?"

I couldn't speak. The wind had been knocked out of me. A triumphant *baaaaa* from Goat echoed through the darkness, followed by the rapid retreat of hoofbeats.

Emma lifted her head. "Eli?" she asked, her voice shrill. "Are you alive?"

"Garghhhhh," I grunted. It was all I could manage.

"Oh, thank God."

The relief in her voice made me stupid. Made me think that maybe it wasn't so bad, being knocked flat on my ass by a psychotic goat. Because now I knew the truth. Underneath all that anger, she didn't want me hurt. She cared.

"What *was* that?" she asked again.

I struggled to get my breath before answering. "That," I panted, "was Goat. As in, Goat's Tavern. Luke found him when he was nothing but a baby, had to bottle feed him and everything. No idea where he came from. Has a nasty habit of knocking people behind the knee. Thinks it's hilarious when they fall."

"He won't think it's so hilarious when I turn him into gloves," Emma said darkly.

"Luke loves him, for reasons that have yet to be determined."

"Oh." She was quiet, considering. "Maybe I'll let him live. *This* time."

Damn, she smelled good. I took a discreet sniff of her hair. The burrito smell wasn't quite as strong as it usually was, though. Pine trees, soap, and a little bit of paint. I shifted onto my back, still holding her close, and she fell against my chest, her leg sandwiched between my thighs. She wiggled, trying to get off me, I assumed, but all she managed to do was rub against my dick in a way that was more likely to get *me* off.

"Don't move," I said through gritted teeth.

She froze. "Did I hurt you?"

My eyes narrowed at her tone, which was far too sweet and innocent to be real. Emma was a lot of things, but sweet wasn't one of them. "You did that on purpose."

"What? What did I do? Do you mean this?" She slid her thigh slowly along the increasingly hard ridge in my jeans. "Is that what you mean?"

I hissed a warning through my teeth.

She did it again.

I rolled, pinning her flat on her back beneath me. I held both her wrists above her head with one hand and leaned in close, until our lips were only an inch apart. So tempting. God, I wanted to kiss her. Wanted to close that miniscule distance and give relief to all these inconvenient feelings.

But I couldn't. It had to be her.

"*This*, Ms. Andrews. This is why I don't want Luke touching you. Yeah, I know I don't have any right to make claims on you, but I'm going to do it anyway." I paused, taking in the sudden flare of heat in her eyes. "And you *like* it. You like that I'm claiming you."

"I don't."

I laughed softly. "Liar."

For a moment we both stopped breathing, both of us frozen as the moment wrapped around us like a blanket. Then she let out a shaky breath.

"Yeah," she whispered.

It was all I could do to stop myself from taking her mouth. I had *promised*.

"Well?" I said roughly. "Are you going to kiss me or not?"

I heard her swallow hard, felt her breasts pitch against me in a sharp inhalation. We were so close I couldn't tell my heartbeat from hers.

She shook her head.

I had expected that, but still the disappointment was nearly unbearable. Her gaze fell to my lips, and she wet her own with the tip of her tongue, and that eased the sting somewhat. She wanted me. She just didn't want the *responsibility* of wanting me. How was it she so readily accepted the care and keeping of everyone around her, but was such a rank coward when it came to caring for her own needs?

That was a conversation for another day. Right now, I needed to get out of there before I broke my promise to her. And to myself.

"Are you sure? That's what you want?" I asked. Fuck, I was *this close* to begging.

"I will *never* kiss you, Eli."

"Suit yourself." I released her wrists, placed my palms flat on the ground bracketing her shoulders, and pushed myself up, careful not to crush her. Once standing, I offered her a hand. She refused, scrambling to her feet without my assistance.

I made for the door, swung it open, and paused. "You're wrong, you know. A kiss like we had, it's special. You know that's true, and there's no sense in pretending otherwise. You wouldn't have teased me like that if you didn't feel the same way. Eventually, you are going to kiss me."

I just hoped waiting for it didn't kill me first.

Chapter 15

Emma

I didn't follow Eli inside. For a long moment I stood in the dim parking lot, debating. My body was still vibrating with a restless energy from the encounter with Eli. Adrenaline, maybe, from my close escape with Goat. Annoyance from being accused of flirting with Luke, as though Eli had any say in the matter. *Horniness*. Might as well call a spade a spade.

Anyway, my fries were cold by now.

I couldn't face cold fries and Eli's smoldering smirk right now. It was too much. Tomorrow. I would come back tomorrow, at a time when I could be sure Eli was on duty and not hanging around the bar, and fix things with Luke.

What I needed right now was to wash off this day and some mindless television to take my mind off Eli and his mouth.

His words continued to ring in my ears the entire drive home. *Eventually, you are going to kiss me.* I ground my teeth in frustration. He was wrong about that. He had to be. I wasn't going to kiss him. This was lust, that's all. Lust couldn't override everything that had gone down between them. The betrayal. The years of nothing. He hadn't...he hadn't even *apologized*. Not once.

Not even the night it all went down, when I had come home from work to find him sitting in my living room. He had told me, bluntly, that he had arrested my dad. There were no explanations. No excuses. No apologies. He had been entirely dispassionate about the whole thing. And I had screamed at him, terrible words, saying that I never wanted to see him again. Even then, he hadn't apologized or explained. He had just nodded and left, like it was nothing to him.

Lust couldn't change that. I would never forget. But if *he* kissed *me*, maybe I could overlook it for a minute.

I turned on the shower, setting the temperature to nearly scalding, and angled my body so the stream of water bore down on the tight knots in my shoulders. The bathroom filled with steam, enveloping me in a warm, damp mist. It felt good, but I still couldn't fully relax. My mind was still in that moment with Eli, our bodies pressed against each other, our mouths only a breath apart.

Damn him.

I scrubbed hard at my hair and body and managed to remove most of the paint remnants. If only it were as easy to remove this inconvenient craving for something—some*one*—that was so wrong for me.

The water was cooling now, and I reluctantly turned it off. I toweled dry, squeezing the excess water from my hair, and followed up with a layer of lotion before slipping into my pajamas.

It was barely nine, but I was clean and cozy. It had been such a long day, and years of pre-dawn mornings selling burritos had conditioned me to go to bed early. Considering all the physical labor I'd suffered through, by all rights I should fall asleep the second my head hit the pillow. I was *exhausted*. Even my eyelids ached.

Instead, I lay in my comfy bed, staring blankly into the darkness, my body aching in a way that had nothing to do with sore muscles and everything to do with rolling around in the grass with Eli Carter. Desire was still coursing through my bloodstream like an electric current. I needed relief. I needed *release*.

Fortunately, I didn't need Eli for release. I could take care of that myself.

I settled more deeply into my soft pillows and tried to relax. I closed my eyes and conjured an image of a rumpled Mr. Darcy walking through a misty field at dawn from *Pride and Prejudice*, my personal favorite way to start a session of self-pleasure. I slipped my hand between the apex of my thighs.

Dark eyes burning into mine. The scrape of rough-hewn wood against my back. My fingers digging into his beard to pull his face to mine—

Oh, God.

My eyes popped open. Mr. Darcy didn't have a beard, and I was fairly certain that was a barn wall I was imagining pressed against my back. It was Eli's dark eyes, Eli's bronzed skin, Eli's mouth claiming mine. I was thinking of Eli. I was thinking of Eli and touching myself.

No. *No, no, no.*

I jumped out of bed like the sheets had caught fire. What was I doing? I couldn't do *that*. It didn't feel wrong, though. It felt...pathetic. I was exhausted and frustrated and horny as hell and this wasn't going to solve any of those problems. I could give myself orgasm after orgasm and it wouldn't touch the ocean-deep well of need I felt for Eli.

Only one thing could do that.

I grabbed my shoes.

Chapter 16

Eli

I had just kicked off my boots and was on my way to the fridge to grab a beer and see what I could throw together for dinner. It had been a long day of work that included a domestic disturbance at seven a.m. Seven was technically before my shift even started, but Billy Combs had chosen that time to finally return home—drunk, of course—and hit his wife for not having breakfast ready for him. There had also been a loose dog to round up, because Hart's Ridge didn't have Animal Control, and several speeding tickets.

The interlude at Goat's Tavern with Emma hadn't helped. All it had done was ratchet up the tension in me until I felt as taut as an arrow on a bowstring. One slight motion would send me flying.

I hadn't eaten anything there, either. Once I realized Emma had left, I'd lost my appetite and headed home. Now it was late, and I was cranky as hell. The last thing I felt like doing was cooking dinner, but my only other option was to order pizza for the second time this week. Hart's Ridge had a lot of things going for it, but takeout at ten p.m. wasn't one of them.

But I could have a beer. Because I wasn't sad. I was so aroused I couldn't think straight, but I wasn't sad. That meant I could have a beer, even if I drank it with a bowl of cereal instead of a real dinner.

At least, that was the plan until I heard a knock on the door.

I looked around the spare living room, wondering if I had imagined it. My house isn't the sort of place people dropped by unexpectedly to hang out. There was only enough seating for myself, which was the exact opposite of where I had grown up, in a house stuffed full of furniture my mom had selected. My dad couldn't bear to part with any of it, no matter how much it fell apart in later years.

I followed a different philosophy when it came to home décor. The furnishings in my one-bedroom house were sparse: a recliner, a coffee table, a television. But the recliner was made from buttery-soft leather, the coffee table was from a local shop that handmade furniture from recycled lumber and iron, and the television was a fifty-five-inch flat screen. I liked nice things, and I liked to treat myself. Who would, if not me?

I didn't even keep an extra chair for guests. Who would sit in it? There aren't a lot of people who want to be close buds with a cop. I had lots of friendly acquaintances, sure. But no one who would come over to hang out. If I wanted to see Luke, I went to the tavern.

So it wasn't a friend at the door, I was certain of that. It wasn't likely to be someone needing my services as a police officer, either. If someone needed something this late at night, they weren't going to waste time driving here to collect me. They were going to call. And if I didn't pick up my work phone, they wouldn't hesitate to call my private number.

The knock came again. Not my imagination. Just in case, I checked my phone on the way to the door. No, I hadn't missed a call or text.

Which meant—

My pulse quickened, pumping blood south in anticipation even before I opened the door. There was only one person I could think of who would show up on my doorstep this late at night, and only one thing she could want.

I jerked the door open, and even though I expected her, even though my body was already preparing, I was still stunned into silence at the sight of Emma on my doorstep. She stood there, pale hair swirling around her shoulders in a gleaming mass, eyes narrowed, arms crossed under her breasts. Looking mad as a wildcat and twice as lethal, pajamas notwithstanding.

My mouth went dry. I couldn't hear over the sudden roaring in my ears. I stepped back, giving her space, hoping she took the gesture as an offer to follow me in.

She did. The moment she stepped over the threshold, I shut the door behind her. Not that I thought she would change her mind, but I didn't want to make the option too appealing, either.

"What are you doing here, Ms. Andrews?"

Her gray eyes flashed at that. It was a dangerous game, egging her on when she was clearly already in a murderous state of mind, but one I couldn't resist playing. Maybe if I got her mad enough, she would finally do something about it.

"I couldn't sleep." The words were an accusation. "I'm exhausted. Usually I can't keep my eyes open past nine. I have to be up at five. But I can't sleep."

Good. I hadn't slept right since the day I'd walked into City Hall and discovered we would be working together. It was only fair that I returned the favor.

I headed for the kitchen. It was the only way to stop myself from dropping to my knees and begging her to put us both out of our misery. Just for tonight. Just so we could get some goddamn sleep. "Do you want something to drink?" I opened the fridge, pulled out two beers.

She shook her head. "I already tried that. It didn't work."

My heart sank into my shoes. If she had been drinking, that would change what happened here tonight. I put one beer back in the fridge and used the counter to pop the cap off the other. "Are you drunk?"

Her face did something odd, twisting into a sympathetic grimace. "No. You know I wouldn't drive drunk, Eli. Especially not after what happened with your dad. I had one beer, hoping it would make me relax. It didn't."

Relief turned my knees wobbly. I leaned against the counter, hoping I somehow managed to look sexy and not like a Victorian lady in need of a fainting couch.

I took a slow pull of my beer. "So here you are. Because you can't sleep. And…you want me to sing you a lullaby?"

The look she gave me was so livid with lust that it would have been funny if it hadn't felt like she kicked me in the heart. The lust I understood, and the anger…well, I supposed I understood that, too. She wanted me. She didn't *want* to want me, and she sure as hell didn't want to admit to any of it.

But that was too bad because I was going to make her say it anyway. She could do with a little personal responsibility for her actions. I wasn't going to allow her to treat tonight like it was just another thing that happened to her, as though she had no role in how it all played out. Once I had done that for her, shouldering the responsibility for something I knew would be unbearable for her to face, but this was different. She could bear it just fine, even if it stung her pride a little.

If she wanted this, if she wanted me, she was going to have to put on her big girl shoes and damn well use her words.

"You know what I want," she said.

I cocked my head to the side and studied her. "I'm not sure I do, to be honest. Why don't you tell me?"

She made a short, frustrated sound. "You won't make this easy on me, will you."

"No."

She took one stride toward me, then abruptly reversed course. She ping-ponged back and forth a few times while I watched, half-amused, half-terrified that she would change her mind. Finally, she stopped, facing me. She was breathing hard, and I doubted it was from physical exertion.

"This has to stop. I can't...I can't live like this. I can't spend my nights staring at the ceiling. I can't walk around all day, like...like..."

"Like what?" My voice was hoarse, shaken. I barely recognized it as my own. "You have to say it, honey."

She closed her eyes, her throat moving as she swallowed hard. "Like I will die if you don't touch me. Like I'm going to catch fire at any moment and you're the only thing that can put me out."

Her eyes opened, burning straight into mine. Two steps and she was in my arms. She dragged her fingertips down the rough stubble of my cheeks, along my jaw, and swept her thumb across my lower lip.

"I need you to make it stop, Eli. I need to fuck you out of my system."

I understood. *For tonight only.* To get it out of our systems once and for all. It wasn't like I was thinking wedding bells and picket fences. I knew forever wasn't on the table. That was fine. Really. Forever didn't exist anyway, in my experience. There was no reason to believe this time would be any different, just because it was Emma.

"I think I can do that," I said.

I lowered my head, but she put a hand to my chest to hold me back.

"This doesn't mean..." Her eyebrows pushed together in a frown. "I hate you, Eli. This won't change that. Does that matter?"

She was giving me an out. Did I want to take it? For a moment I asked myself, quite seriously, if maybe it *did* matter. If maybe this feeling like someone had stabbed me in the gut with a red-hot poker was a sign that I was in over my head...and in over my heart.

The answer was no, it didn't matter. At least, not enough. Nothing mattered enough to stop this from happening. Besides, I had heard *I love you* before. It was generally followed by leaving. It was the last thing my mom had said to me, and it hadn't made one bit of difference in what happened next. So why couldn't *I hate you* be followed by sex? It felt right, in the twisted recesses of my heart. It felt like something I could live with.

As opposed to walking away from Emma, which was something I didn't think I could bear. It was unreasonable to even suggest it, now, with her soft skin under my fingers and her scent filling my lungs. I couldn't say no to this. I didn't even want to, no matter how much it broke me.

"I don't care," I said, which wasn't a lie so much as it wasn't the truth.

She pulled my face toward hers and claimed my mouth. Like the kiss we had shared before, it wasn't gentle. I kissed her hard and deep, knowing that tonight was the last time. Come tomorrow, there would be no more kisses.

But I wasn't going to think about that right now, because right now Emma was in my arms and that made it hard to even consider future regrets. And I sure as hell wasn't going to waste my only time with her backed up against a kitchen counter. Kitchen counters were for lovers who had all the time in the world, for slow, lazy mornings of kissing and sex intermingling with pancakes and coffee. Kitchen counters weren't for us. No, we needed a bed, where I could spread her out and make a feast of her.

I cupped her butt with both hands and boosted her up. She wrapped her long legs around my waist. Somehow I navigated us down the hallway to my bedroom, my lips never once leaving hers.

I carefully laid her down on the bed and tried to unwind myself from her limbs, but she clung to me, keeping me close. The unconscious vulnerability of it made my chest squeeze tight. But I wanted—no, *needed*—her naked, and that wasn't going to happen if she didn't let go of me for at least a moment.

"Clothes off," I said.

She nodded, releasing me, and pulled her T-shirt off over her head, revealing perky tits just the right size for my hands. No bra. The sight tempted my mouth, but if I started that I might never stop, and she wasn't near naked enough for that yet. I pulled off her Converse sneakers and socks. Her toenails were unpainted, which didn't surprise me in the least. She didn't strike me as having a whole lot of extra time for things like pedicures. But it did something to me, seeing her unpainted toes. It felt intimate, somehow. Like I was seeing something not everyone had the privilege of seeing.

I grabbed her pajama bottoms by their elastic waistband and pulled them down her legs. Plain black cotton underwear, sexy as hell on her, although I didn't think that was her intention. I grinned, putting it all together. Pajamas. No bra, serviceable underwear. This truly wasn't a premeditated booty call.

"Is something funny?" she asked, clearly annoyed that I had stopped.

"I'm imagining you at home, in bed, seething because you can't stop thinking about me. You were in your pajamas, weren't you? You were in such a hurry to get here that you didn't even change first. Just pulled on shoes."

"So what?"

"Hm." I ran my thumb under the seam of her panties, tracing the line from her hip bone down the crease between her thigh and that lovely place my dick was aching to be. Her breath hitched in a very gratifying way. "Tell me something. Did you touch yourself? Just a little. Before you realized it wasn't enough. You needed the real thing."

"I—" Her cheeks flushed.

"You did!" I was absolutely delighted about that. Too delighted. The image of her touching herself, thinking of me, made my dick so hard it hurt. *Enough of that*. I had a job to do. "You won't regret this. You can hate me tomorrow, regret that I exist in the same world as you, but you won't regret *this*. I'll give you what you need."

With that, I hooked her underwear with one finger, tugged them off, and tossed them aside. And then...I *looked*.

Emma Andrews was naked in my bed.

Her hair fanned out across my pillow like a halo. He didn't know where to start. With those perfect breasts, tipped by sweetest petal-pink nipples I had ever seen? Or lower, with the golden-brown triangle at the apex of her thighs? *Yes, there*. My mouth watered.

I put a knee on the bed next to her hip and kissed her, threading my fingers through her silky hair as I pressed my hips against hers, letting her feel my weight and how hard

I was. How much I ached for her. I was still fully clothed, except for my shoes, and it drove me nearly insane to feel all that warm, soft skin separated from me by only a layer of fabric. That simple layer of fabric was the only thing keeping my restraint in check, the only thing that kept me from taking her now without foreplay.

For a moment I reconsidered. Was foreplay even necessary right now? We had had *years* of foreplay, even if we had barely understood it at the time. All those little touches, stolen glances, from the moment I had seen her in a bikini when she was fifteen and realized she wasn't a child anymore. And then my dick had promptly hardened, informing me that neither was I. Those eight long years of being invisible to her had only made me hungrier.

But I only had tonight. I was going to do this right, make it last, take her every way I could.

I shifted lower to kiss the alley between her breasts, then lower still to her belly. My lips curved in a smile, remembering how she had used me for a ladder. I had fantasized about this moment, and now that it was a reality, I wasn't going to waste the opportunity. I kissed her there, swirled the tip of my tongue in the indentation of her navel. She made a sound, a shocked giggle, and I had never felt so proud of myself. Emma wasn't one to giggle. I lifted my head for a moment and grinned at her.

"Couldn't resist," I said.

Her fingers grazed my cheek in an oddly affectionate touch before her hand dropped to her side again. "I don't want you to resist anything."

Good. Because I wouldn't. I couldn't.

She was panting heavily as I moved farther down, her stomach rising and falling with each labored breath. I paused there, at the most intimate part of her, savoring the moment.

My dick hurt.

My heart hurt.

And there was nowhere else I would rather be.

I made room for my shoulders between her thighs, pressing them wider so I had better access to the heart of her. I slid a finger gently down her center and then pressed deeper. She was wet with desire. *For me.* Only for me.

I lowered my head and tasted her deeply while continuing to tease her with my fingers. She gasped, her breaths coming in short, hard pants. Then suddenly—and far too soon—she gave a sharp cry, her back arched off the bed, and I felt her internal muscles clench in a rhythmic spasm around my fingers. It was a miracle I didn't come in my pants right then and there.

She fell back, breasts rising and falling rapidly, muscles limp. She started to roll away, but I grabbed her hips. I raised my head and pierced her with a long stare. Hell, no. I had waited years for this. Waited fucking *years* to taste her. We weren't done yet. I was just getting started.

"I wasn't finished, Ms. Andrews," I said sternly, and was pleased when she shivered.

"Sorry. It's been...it's been a while."

"I'm not finished," I repeated. "Be a good girl and let me enjoy my dessert."

And lowered my head.

The first touch made her tremble and curl into herself just a little. Her orgasm had left her sensitive. I shifted, keeping my stroke gentle, giving her time to recover. I was a patient man, and for this, for her, I had all the time in the world. She was delicious, even better than my imagination had prepared me for.

I lapped softly until she let me know she was ready for more. Her hips canted, seeking more friction from my mouth. I complied, gripping her more firmly, increasing the pace. She dug her fingers through my hair, holding my head close to her as another orgasm sent her internal muscles pulsing. Pleasure washed through me, more intense than I had ever experienced without an orgasm of my own.

She collapsed, boneless, and slowly I pulled away. God, she looked beautiful there in my bed. Peaceful. She had arrived on my doorstep angry and tense, but now she was sated. All the fight had seemed to drain from her with that first orgasm, and the second had sent her to euphoria.

"Don't fall asleep," I begged, shucking my pants and shirt in record time.

"Not asleep," she murmured. She blinked slowly and then her eyes widened as she took me in. Her gaze raked over me and she smiled. "Mmm."

I wanted to tell her no, that she couldn't look at me like that. That if she looked at me like that, I might get ideas that she wanted to keep me. But I liked it too much to tell her to stop. Like everything else with Emma, the pain was more pleasurable than the emptiness of nothing.

I grabbed a condom from the nightstand, ripped the foil packet open, and rolled it over my aching length. I joined her on the bed, pressing her back to the mattress, every inch of her bare skin touching my bare skin. *Finally*. She parted her legs, making room for me, and my erection settled there against her warm, slick skin.

Too much. Fuck, it was too much. I stopped, momentarily overwhelmed. I shivered and dropped my forehead to hers, trying to ground myself in the moment. It was all right. There was nothing to fear here.

"Eli," she whispered. She squeezed my ass, urging me to move.

As if I would deny her anything. Ever. I didn't hesitate. I bucked forward, sheathing myself completely in her tight, wet heat. I wanted to go slow, to savor, to stretch this moment out as long as I was able, but I was past all that now. Past restraint. Past patience.

I could feel her release building again. I was familiar with it now, the way her muscles went taught, the way her hands fluttered as she searched for something to hold on to. I understood the feeling. It was comforting that she, too, was overwhelmed and in need of grounding.

I couldn't hold back any longer. She shuddered beneath me, nails digging into my back, her internal muscles pulsing around me as she climaxed, pulling me deeper. Blood roared in my ears as the last vestiges of my control snapped completely. I pounded into her, conscious only of this need to finish. To finally have her, completely. Pleasure burst through me like an explosion, a single word ripped from my throat.

"*Emma.*"

Chapter 17

Emma

Home.

It wasn't so much a word as it was a feeling that engulfed me before I was fully conscious. It was the scent of spicy aftershave and generic shampoo, a combination so intensely familiar that my life flashed in a series of hazy, dream-like scenes. Eli spinning me in a circle at the homecoming dance. Eli grabbing my waist, hauling me back when I leaned too far over the safety bar on the Ferris wheel. Eli crawling into bed with me the night my mother died, holding me while a never-ending stream of tears soaked my pillow. *Eli, Eli, Eli*. His name was a drumbeat matching the rhythm of my heart.

I opened my eyes.

It took a moment of fumbling in the dark for my alarm to realize that I was not in my own house. Something warm brushed against my cheek and the incessant beeping stopped. The mattress shifted as he stood, and then there was the soft sound of bare feet padding across the wood floor. A second later the hall light turned on, the light muted enough that it didn't hurt my eyes. I watched him return to me and ached a little at how beautiful he was. He looked like something Michelangelo had sculpted, but instead of cold marble, he was warm flesh and muscle.

"Hey." He sat next to me, making me roll toward him slightly when the mattress dipped from his weight. "Are you awake?"

"Yes. What time is it?" I rubbed my eyes.

"Quarter to five."

I sat up. Perfect. That would give me time to get home, shower, and meet Cesar. "Early day for you?"

He shook his head. "My shift doesn't start until nine. You said you needed to be up by five."

I paused in the act of pulling my shirt on over my head and looked at him. "You set your alarm for me?"

"You fell asleep hard and fast after"—he made a vague hand gesture—"so I didn't want to wake you. I figured it would be better to let you sleep."

Had I told him what time I had to be up? I didn't remember that, but I wasn't surprised that *he* did. Typical Eli. He could always be depended on to do the right thing. Set the alarm so I would be up when I needed to be up. Run for mayor when no one else was interested in the job. It wasn't anything new with him; he had always been that way, from the day they had met in kindergarten, when I had forgotten my lunch so he had given me half his sandwich and a cookie. Sturdy. Dependable.

Galling.

How could the traits that drew me to him in the first place be the exact same traits that caused our irreparable rift? How had I not known that he would arrest my dad? How—

Well. I hadn't known. That was all there was to it. I had been distraught when I went to Eli with what I had discovered. Not thinking straight. Shock did that to a person.

I hadn't known. I repeated that to myself.

I shimmied into my pajama pants, pushing the thoughts down into the dark hole of my mind where they belonged. I wasn't going to replay it over and over again. What good would that do?

"Thanks," I said. "For setting the alarm, I mean."

He regarded me quizzically. "Right. Because that's what we were talking about. What else would you mean?"

Thank God he wasn't privy to my inner thoughts. "I don't know. For the mind-blowing sex, maybe?"

Eli collapsed backward onto the bed, grabbing his chest like the shock had given him a heart attack. "Did you really just say that?"

"Are you saying you *didn't* think it was mind-blowing?"

I didn't think my pride could take that. It wasn't as though I had never had good sex before. I had. Really good sex, even. But this…this was different. It had been so much *more* than I was used to. More heat. More intensity. More orgasms. Three, to be precise, which was two more than usual for me.

It had been more than mind-blowing. It had been soul-shattering.

I hadn't realized that sex could be so…so *intimate*. That it could be more than two sweaty bodies seeking to give and receive physical pleasure. Well, I had known, technically. I understood, in a very mechanical sort of way, that sex was, by definition, an intimate act. But I had never *felt* it in that way before. Had never experienced that kind of intimacy for myself. Until Eli had called my name.

That was the moment when sex had crossed over from being simply *more* to being *too much*. My chest had felt like it might crack in two, and tears had slipped from my eyes before I could stop them. Fortunately, Eli hadn't seemed to notice.

It had been so raw. So terrifying.

I shook my head, trying to clear the thoughts away. Better not to think about the soul-shattering parts. I would focus on the mind-blowing aspect. The orgasms. The things that felt good. Ignore the scary feelings that had tagged along for the ride.

He still hadn't answered my question, which was unforgivable. "Well?" I demanded.

"Yes, the sex was mind-blowing." Eli traced a seam on the white duvet. It was one of those down comforters meant to have a washable cover, but he had left it bare. It was a strange dichotomy, because the sheets were actually very nice. The softest I had ever slept on, in fact. I wondered about that, about the decadent sparseness of his entire house. Everything was for the comfort and enjoyment of exactly one person. There wasn't room for anyone else here.

"We should do it again sometime," he said.

"Okay."

We stared at each other.

"All right," he said slowly. Then he cleared his throat. "Sorry, but what is it, exactly, we're agreeing to?"

I let out the breath I didn't know I was holding in a startled laugh. "You're the one who propositioned *me*, Eli. So I guess the question is, what, exactly, are you propositioning?"

He shifted, pulling the duvet over his lap. I watched him with avid interest. He was still naked, and until this very moment, he had seemed entirely comfortable with his nakedness.

"You know," he said vaguely.

My words from the night before came back to me with acute clarity. My words...and his response. *You know what I want*, I had said. If he had, he wouldn't admit it. *I don't think I do*, he had replied. *Why don't you tell me?*

Now it appeared our roles were reversed. *He* was the one with the dark desire that he loathed to give words to, and *I* was the one who was going to gleefully pull it out of him. Oh, yes, I was. I nearly rubbed my hands together and chortled like an old-timey villain in a black-and-white movie.

It wasn't hard to guess what he wanted, and why it bothered him so much to admit it. This was straight-and-narrow Eli, after all. The man who followed the law to the letter, even if that meant arresting his best friend's dad.

The man who always buttoned his shirt to the very top, even if it choked him.

He had probably never had sex without the requisite three dates first. It must chap his hide to realize he wanted meaningless, commitment-free sex, and with *me* of all people. To realize he was just as human as everyone else. Just as fallible. Just as needy.

What a goddamn delightful turn of events this was.

"I don't think I do know what you want, Eli," I said, enjoying throwing his words back in his face. "Why don't you tell me?"

He scowled. "You're enjoying this."

"Immensely." I beamed.

The muscle in his jaw twitched, but he remained stubbornly silent.

"Come on," I said. "If we're going to do this, we need all our cards on the table. There is too much history between us. Too much *bad* history. Let's not set ourselves up for an unnecessary misunderstanding."

"It wasn't *all* bad."

I blinked, remembering how I had felt waking up in his bed, in his arms. The thoughts that had consumed me before I was fully awake. It wasn't that I had forgotten the bad things. But in that brief, hazy moment, the bad things had been outweighed by all the good that had come before.

"No," I said softly. "It wasn't all bad."

"But you're right. We're already set up as opponents in the mayoral race. A misunderstanding involving sex might cause World War III. Cards on the table, then."

I waited. When he didn't follow that statement up with putting his metaphorical cards on the table, I raised my eyebrows. "Use your words, Eli," I coaxed. "It's easy. All you have to say is, *Emma, I want no-strings-attached, meaningless sex until one or both of us decides we're done with it*. See? Easy."

"Right. That's what I'm asking for." He made a sound of disgust. "Because that's what this is, and there's no sense in pretending it's something else."

The anger in his voice took me aback. Was it the meaningless sex that he found distasteful, or the meaningless sex *with me*? "We don't have to do this. If you don't want to. If you have, I don't know, moral qualms about sleeping with someone you're not technically even dating."

"Oh, we're doing this, all right."

"Eli—"

He hauled me against him, cutting off my words with a hard, brief kiss. "We're doing this."

My lips tingled. I liked that. It made other parts of me tingle, too. "All right."

"But I do have strings."

Of course he did. "All right. Let's hear it."

"First, while this is happening with us, we don't see other people. We're not dating, but that doesn't mean this isn't a relationship, even if it is kind of twisted. I don't juggle, and I don't share."

I blew out a sigh. That was a relief, actually. And not only because the thought of him with someone else made my insides feel like someone had taken a rusty chainsaw to my stomach. I didn't want to see anyone else, either. Who had time for that?

"We're on the same page, there. What else?"

"We have an end date: the election. It makes sense, because after that, we won't have to see each other anymore. If you want out before that..." He paused, looking away. "When you're done, you tell me. To my face. None of this texting shit. I'll make it easy on you, don't worry about that. Just...don't disappear on me."

Like everyone else had. The unspoken words hung in the air. My chest tightened. It would be easier if we didn't know each other so well. If I hadn't known where all his scars were, and where to stick the knife to cause the most pain.

I took his chin between my index finger and thumb, turning his face toward me. "Look at me, Eli. I will *never* leave without telling you. Okay?"

He swallowed, the lines of his throat moving. "Okay." He pushed my hand away and glanced at the clock. "You should get going. It's past five."

I let out a little yelp. I was going to be late. Hastily, I shoved my feet into my sneakers, not bothering to tie them. "So, we have a deal? We're doing this?"

He grinned. "Hell yeah. We're doing this."

Chapter 18

Eli

I collapsed backward on the bed. My heart was pounding, my hands shaking with adrenaline, as though I had wrestled one of the black bears that populated the mountains surrounding Hart's Ridge instead of simply telling Emma Andrews that yes, I wanted some sort of twisted enemies-with-benefits relationship with her.

I was fucked. I was *so* fucked, but at least I was also going to *get* fucked, which eased some of the sting a little.

And now she was gone. She had let herself out, telling me to go back to sleep since I didn't have to be at work for another three hours or so. As if sleep was even possible, after that.

My stomach growled, reminding me that I had skipped dinner last night. First, because she had stormed into my house demanding sex. And secondly, because after receiving the requested sex, she had rolled onto her side, trapping my arm underneath her, and promptly fallen asleep. I could have woken her up, but if I had done that, she would have gone home. I hadn't wanted her to leave. I hadn't wanted to be alone with my thoughts and What It All Meant.

Hell no.

So I had stayed still, mostly awake, hungry for food and hungry for her. I had lied to myself last night, telling myself that once was enough. It *had* to be enough, because it was all I could have. But I had wanted her for too long to be satisfied with just once. Too long, and too quietly. I hadn't let myself be truly aware of the longing since the moment eight years ago when she told me she never wanted to see me again. I had buried it deep. Until last night.

It hadn't been enough. It was like giving a man a single potato chip after years of starving in a desert. All it had done was make me hungrier. The hunger was so much a part of me now that I didn't think I could ever be satiated.

But it would be a hell of a lot of fun trying.

If it didn't kill me.

It could go either way.

I would think about that later. Or, better yet, never. Right now, I needed breakfast.

Breakfast, fortunately, was something I excelled at. I might not have the energy or the capacity to take care of myself after a long shift, but I always started the day off right. Back when feeding myself had been a simple matter of self-preservation, after my mom had finally left for the last time and my dad was either too hung over or too drunk, depending on the time of day, breakfast had consisted of cold cereal or frozen waffles. As a seven-year-old, I hadn't known how to crack an egg, much less operate a stove.

But that had changed after my dad died. That was when it really hit home that I was on my own. No one was ever going to take care of me again, but then, it had been such a long time since anyone really had that it didn't truly matter. I could take care of myself, and dammit, I would do it *well*.

After last night's activities, I was craving something hearty. Quiche, with a side of fruit, and maybe some bacon, too. Quiche was usually something I reserved for days off, since between the prep work and baking, it was a time-consuming endeavor. There were perks to waking up before dawn to make sure Emma got where she needed to go. Today, I had the time.

I briefly considered ham and spinach before settling on bacon, white cheddar, and scallion, which meant that I was doubling up on bacon, but dammit, I didn't care. Last night I had slept with Emma. Been *inside* her. Let her rip out a piece of my soul to take with her as she went on her merry way. A little comfort food was in order. For me, there was nothing more comforting than bacon. Except maybe lasagna, which wasn't a breakfast food. So bacon it was.

I grabbed the pre-made piecrust and package of shredded cheese from the fridge. I fed myself well, but I wasn't above cutting corners. For breakfast quiche, anyway. When it came time for the Fourth of July Pie Baking Contest, I would be making a lard-and-butter crust from scratch guaranteed to melt in even the coldest mouth.

The crust was blind baking, the scallions chopped, and the bacon sizzling in my cast-iron pan when my phone rang. I glanced at the screen and sighed. I didn't recognize the number other than noting the local area code, but as the only full-time officer assigned to Hart's Ridge, I didn't have the luxury of screening calls. Half the town called my personal number rather than the police number, anyway.

Still, calling my personal cell about police business before working hours wasn't something I wanted to encourage, either. I hit accept and then speaker. "Yeah?"

"Officer Carter, this is Jacob Bronson." When I didn't respond, because I thought it more pertinent to tend to the bacon, he continued dryly, "You remember, the man financing your campaign for mayor?"

I rolled my eyes, grateful that Bronson hadn't made this a video call. "Right. What can I do for you?"

"We need to rethink our strategy. This election might not be as easy to win as we thought."

We. The word made my skin crawl. I didn't want to be part of any *we* that involved Jacob Bronson. The man was slime.

"Emma is doing a better job as acting mayor than I expected. She was running all over town yesterday, buttering up the business owners, making promises. I'm thinking we're going to need to change tactics a bit."

As far as I was concerned, my only tactic was to lose. I'd be damned if I let Bronson get in the way of that. "What did you have in mind?"

"New posters, to start with. A catchy slogan that reminds the good people of Hart's Ridge what you stand for. The rest...well, doing a bit more hand-shaking wouldn't hurt."

"Posters. Yeah, okay." I cracked four eggs into a large bowl and whisked them into a golden yellow froth, then added milk, cheese, scallions, and spices. All the posters in the world wouldn't change the fact that Emma was damn good at her new job. "What's the slogan?"

"Still working that out," Bronson said vaguely.

"Okay, well, you let me know." Then, not for any real reason other than a desperate need to end the phone call, I added, "Have to cut this short. Duty calls." That duty being to my stomach, but there was no reason for Bronson to know that.

"Right," Bronson said. "We'll talk later."

I hung up the phone and squinted at it questioningly. Those last words sounded like a threat, but maybe that was because the thought of spending even five minutes in Bronson's company was unpleasant. I shrugged and tossed the phone aside.

Last night I'd had amazing sex, this morning I was going to have amazing quiche, and I wasn't going to let Bronson ruin any of that. It didn't matter, anyway.

Not even Jacob Bronson could stop Emma from winning this election.

Chapter 19

Emma

The red wand made its inexorable sweep around the clock face, counting down the seconds to nine a.m., also known as my impending doom.

Mistakes had been made. I had slept with Eli last night, that was mistake number one. Agreeing to make a regular thing of it this morning, that was mistake number two. Right now it didn't feel like a mistake, but that was because my body was still humming happily from the orgasms. Once that wore off, I would see the error of my ways. Sleeping with your ex-best-friend who arrested your dad was always a mistake. That was just common sense.

But more relevant to the nauseous feeling in my stomach was mistake number three: Agreeing to be mayor.

It was officially my first day as Acting Mayor without Mr. Whittaker right there next to me, making sure I didn't screw anything up too badly. Last week I had shadowed him, attending office hours in between serving up burritos, scrubbing the iron lamp posts, and turning my home into a bed and breakfast. It was a lot to take in, and not a lot of time to learn it.

Mostly I had stayed quiet, listening intently as Mr. Whittaker resolved one neighbor dispute after another—and there were a *lot*. Each time, Mr. Whittaker would grab one of the thick volumes that lined the bookshelf, miraculously open it to the exact page he needed, and proclaim, "The regulation is clear as day." Boom, problem solved.

But I couldn't solve problems by pointing at a law or regulation—and there was, in fact, a difference between the two, according to Mr. Whittaker—because I didn't have any idea what the law actually was. According to Mr. Whittaker, there was a regulation for everything. That didn't make me feel any better about it. If anything, that made it worse. How was I supposed to obey the law if I didn't know what it was?

"The solution to every problem is right here," Mr. Whittaker had said, giving the bookshelf a fond pat like it was an old friend. "Some folks might not be too happy with it, but the law is finite. It's not personal. Just look to the regulations, Emma. You'll be all right."

The growing panic in my stomach had told me I wouldn't be all right at all. Unlike Mr. Whittaker, I didn't have a decade of experience as mayor, and if being a good mayor meant reading all those books…well, I had never met a textbook that didn't put me to sleep. If my mediocrity at school had taught me one thing, it was that my brain simply refused to process boring words.

Hart's Ridge was *screwed*.

The minute hand hit the two. It was now 9:10. I let out a slow, unsteady breath. Maybe no one would show up? Maybe—

My hopes were crushed by a knock at the door. A spike of anxiety laced up my spine. "Come in," I said, hoping I didn't sound as nervous as I felt.

The door opened, and I breathed a sigh of relief at seeing two familiar faces. Mr. McKinley and Mrs. López were neighbors on Applewood Lane, only a block off Main Street, and both had been frequent customers of my Airstream. They had always seemed like perfectly nice and reasonable people, not the kind who would pitch a screaming fit over how frequently a neighbor mowed his lawn, like Mrs. Gracen had last week. My mouth had dropped open at the sight of a fifty-year-old woman throwing a tantrum like a four-year-old, but Mr. Whittaker had calmly pointed to the ordinance requiring lawns to be less than eight inches in height and sent her on her way, armed with the knowledge to vanquish her neighbors.

"Good morning, Emma," Mrs. López said cheerfully. "Or should I call you Mayor Andrews?"

I straightened. *Mayor Andrews*. A title for a goddamn grownup if ever there was one. If I was going to convince people I could do the job, I needed to act the part. Eli exuded authority. People believed in him. People needed to believe in me, too, even if I was wearing jeans and a T-shirt instead of a uniform.

"Mayor Andrews is fine," I said, leaning into my new role. "What can I do for you?"

"You can tell Greg here to stop being an ornery old jackass and mind his business," Mrs. López said, her pleasant tone at odds with her words. "I would appreciate it."

I blinked.

"Or how about you tell Alexis that the eyesore she's building in her backyard *is* my business, and affects my property as much as hers," Mr. McKinley snapped. "Seeing as I have to look at it."

I blinked again.

"Have you tried looking somewhere else?" Mrs. López's voice now dripped with fake sweetness.

Mr. McKinley's face turned so red I was worried he would explode.

"Why don't we start from the beginning?" I cut in hastily. "Mrs. López, what are you building, exactly?"

"A treehouse. In a tree that happens to be in *my* backyard, which means he has no say in it."

"The trunk is in your yard, by no more than an inch, but half the branches hang on my side of the fence, and you know damn well the roots have spread onto my property. I think that means I have some say in it, and I say it has to go." He tilted his head in the direction of the bookcase. "I don't recall seeing a permit for building the treehouse. How about you tell us what the law says about that. That's what Mayor Whittaker would do."

He was right about that. Of course there was a law or ordinance to regulate treehouses, and of course Mr. Whittaker would have found the it in no time. But I didn't even know where to begin. A bead of sweat ran down my neck. There had to be another way.

Not just another way. A *better* way.

Because the law would decide that either Mrs. López was right or Mr. McKinley, and if one of them was right, then one of them had to be wrong. What would that solve, really? They would still have to be neighbors. Anyway, a treehouse should make people happy, not mad.

I had the feeling something else was going on here. On more than one occasion, I had witnessed Mr. McKinley playing tea party with his granddaughter, Ava, on his wraparound front porch. Men who willingly wore pink feather boas in public to make their granddaughters happy were not the kind to crusade against a frickin' treehouse, for heaven's sake. Maybe I could appeal to him as a grandfather.

"Mrs. López, isn't Daniel around the same age as Ava?" I asked.

She nodded. "They were in the same class in preschool last year. I'm sure he would love to have Ava over to play in the treehouse when it's done," she added with a sideways glance at Mr. McKinley.

Mr. McKinley frowned.

"Wouldn't Ava like that?" I prodded. "She's with you a lot during the summer, isn't she?" Schools were closed for the summer, and I knew Ava spent many of her days with her grandfather while her parents worked.

"Well, I would have thought so," he admitted. "But she's upset about the whole thing. It's her favorite tree, and she's always thought of it as hers. There's a fence separating our properties, but as the tree grew, we had to take out that section of the fence to give it more space, so it looks like it's no-man's-land, though as I said, it's on their property by an inch. With a tree house on their side of the fence, it won't be *her* tree anymore."

"Por Dios!" Mrs. López said. "You are telling me that you are doing the bidding of a child?"

"She cried," Mr. McKinley said.

"She's five. She will stop crying once she sees how fun it is to play in the treehouse."

My gaze darted back and forth as they argued. I was enjoying myself now. It reminded me of my favorite part of running the food truck: Talking to people, hearing about the minutia of their lives. I leaned back in my chair and stared at the ceiling. There wasn't a fan, but it wasn't a very difficult problem, now that I understood the heart of it.

"Hmm," I said.

They stopped squabbling and looked at me expectantly.

"Maybe the solution isn't *no* treehouse. Maybe it's a *bigger* treehouse. A treehouse that encompasses branches on both properties and can be accessed from either side of the fence. It's not Ava's tree, Mr. McKinley, but maybe it can still *feel* like her tree if everyone is willing to share it." I turned to Mrs. López. "Would that be agreeable to you, Mrs. López?"

She smiled. "I think Daniel and Ava would like that solution. What do you think, Greg?"

"It's a deal. Hell, I'll even help Adam build it." He stood. "Thank you for your time, Mayor Andrews."

"It was a pleasure."

I walked them to the door and watched them walk down the hallway together. Once they turned the corner, I did a celebratory hip shimmy. I did it! My first official day as mayor was a success. I—

"Ma'am."

I let out a surprised shriek and spun on my toes. "Sorry, Mr. Billings. I didn't see you there. I was just—"

He held up a sheet of paper, cutting me off. "I'm being fined two hundred and fifty dollars for my lawn being over eight inches. Two hundred and fifty dollars! Now, if I had that kind of money, don't you think I'd have had someone out to cut my damn lawn? How am I supposed to pay this?"

I stared at the notice he was waving in my face and swallowed hard. I had the feeling this was the result of Mrs. Gracen's tantrum last week. As Mr. McKinley had pointed out, the law was very clearly on her side of things. Which meant poor Mr. Billings was in the wrong to the tune of two hundred and fifty dollars.

"I can't mow it myself on account of the heart attack I had last year," he went on, driving home the guilt with every word. "I live on social security, and the monthly check isn't enough to cover a luxury like lawn mowing. Not if I want to eat and keep a roof over my head. What am I supposed to do? And before you suggest I lean on the kindness of neighbors, let me remind you that my neighbor is Bunny Gracen."

"I—I don't know." But that wasn't good enough, and I knew it. A mayor *had* to know. I squared my shoulders. "I'll mow your lawn myself. Tomorrow. And I'll have the fine canceled." I could cancel town fines as mayor, couldn't I? The answer was probably in one of those damned books Mr. Whittaker was so fond of.

His face softened. "That's kind of you to offer, but it isn't a real solution. You think I'm the only one in Hart's Ridge with a wrecked body and worrisome bank account? The high school kids take care of us when it's time to shovel snow in the winter, but we're on our own in the summer, and there's at least a few dozen of us. What are you gonna do, mow all our lawns? It's not possible. Not even you, Emma."

I didn't know what he meant by that, *not even me*, but I wasn't going to waste time worrying it through. The gears were already turning in my brain. *The high school kids*. I had a wonderful, horrible feeling that the solution had been right there in front of us for *years*, and it wasn't Ordinance 2014-199.

Back when I attended John Hart High School, there had been a requirement of ten hours of community service to graduate. To help facilitate that, a school club had formed to shovel snow off sidewalks and driveways for Hart's Ridge citizens who met certain income and need requirements.

"Why don't you come in and have a seat?" I said. "I think I might have an idea."

He gave me a doubtful look. "I suppose it won't hurt to hear you out. And I'll take you up on canceling the fine. If you could just put that in writing, I would appreciate it."

I laughed. "Of course." I took my seat behind the oak desk and Mr. Billings sat across from me. "The high school kids you mentioned. Is that the club for community service?"

"Right. That's it. But they don't do lawn service, just snow," he said patiently.

"Just because they haven't before doesn't mean they can't." I pulled up the school website on my laptop. There was an ancient desktop, but it was slow, so I only used it when I had to.

After a bit of searching, I found the page for the community service club. "It looks like Celia Smith is still the organizer. I'll send her an email." I typed out a quick message, included my phone number, and hit send. "There. I don't know when I'll hear back, since school is closed for the summer, but I'll let you know the second I hear—"

My phone rang, startling me. "Good morning, this is Mayor Andrews." The words sounded funny coming from my own mouth.

"Emma! How are you, honey?" Mrs. Smith didn't wait for a response before plowing forward. "See, the thing is, we don't do lawn service. Just snow. Do you know how many people have heart attacks every year shoveling snow?"

"No," I said. "How many?"

There was a pause. "A lot."

"Oh. Okay."

"That's why we count it as a community service. Now, I'm not against adding lawn service, but there has to be a need for it. A benefit to the community members."

"I believe it would help the same community members who aren't physically or financially able to clear their own sidewalks and driveways," I said. "Heart attacks can happen when you mow the lawn. And, um"—I Googled frantically—"heatstroke. Plus there's a fine if your lawn is taller than eight inches, so that makes it even worse."

"Two hundred and fifty dollars!" Mr. Billings bellowed.

"What was that?" Mrs. Smith said. "Who said that?"

"Mr. Billings. He's in my office right now. He needs his lawn mowed for the same reasons he needs his snow shoveled. And now he's looking at a fine of two-hundred-and-fifty dollars."

"Goodness. That changes things." Mrs. Smith heaved a sigh. "I don't see any reason why we can't incorporate lawn service into the community service club. I'm sure some students would love to get those hours done before senior year begins. I'll get the details ironed out and touch base with you on Friday. Hopefully we can send someone out to Mr. Billings this weekend. How does that sound?"

"Fantastic!" I shouted. "I mean, that would be great. Thank you, Mrs. Smith."

I hung up the phone and grinned at Mr. Billings, who nodded. "Well, that was easy. Don't know why no one thought to try that before."

"Oh." I deflated slightly. That was me, coming to the rescue with an obvious solution. "Right."

Mr. Billings winked at me. "Don't worry, kiddo. You *did* think to try that, that's what matters. You have my vote in July."

Normally, I would have murdered just about anyone who called me kiddo, but in this case I figured I would make an exception. "Thank you."

I breathed a long sigh of relief as Mr. Billings exited my office, closing the door behind him. The clock read 10:50. Ten more minutes, and office hours would be over and I could call my first official day a success.

Because it *was* a success, which honestly surprised the hell out of me. I was out of my depth, and I still only had the faintest grasp of the differences between laws, regulations, and ordinances, much less when they actually applied. But I had solved two problems today. I had made lives better, and that was so much bigger than lamp posts.

I could do this job. I could really do it. Maybe I could even be great at it.

I *wanted* to be great at it. I would be, some day.

I just had to beat Eli first.

Chapter 20

Eli

Is sometime now?

I wiped the condensation from the screen and stared at my phone for several long moments. Leave it to Emma to text now. She could have texted during any of the five hundred times I had checked my phone that day, but of course she hadn't. I had been distracted all day, still buzzing from the orgasm from the night before, afraid I would miss whatever small window of opportunity she was willing to give me if I set my phone down for even a second. But the text never came.

Fine. Honestly, that was exactly what I had expected. We had just had sex yesterday, after all, and parted this morning. She wasn't needy like me. I figured she could probably go at least forty-eight hours without wanting me again. Maybe even a week—although for the sake of my balls, I truly hoped not.

Around nine I had finally given up. I had jumped in the shower, carefully placing my phone on the sink—because even though I told himself it wasn't going to happen, I clung to a tiny sliver of hope.

And now, when my hair was full of shampoo, she had texted.

Is this a booty call, Ms. Andrews? I replied. And held my breath.

Three dots appeared, wavering, then disappearing altogether. *Shit.* I shouldn't have pushed it with calling her Ms. Andrews. I started typing an apology when the dots appeared again. My torso hanging out of the shower curtain, soap dripping down my neck, I stared at those dots as though they were the answer to the universe. What the hell was she typing, the next great American novel?

The dots disappeared again. I groaned.

And then—

Yes.

One word, but it was the only word I needed.

I'll be there in twenty, I typed back. I wasn't about to give her a chance to change her mind by letting her come to me. No way. If she drove here, every red light would give her a reason to come to her senses.

I was out of the shower and halfway dressed before I remembered there was still shampoo in my hair. Annoyed, I shucked my jeans and turned the water back on. It was cold now, but maybe that was a good thing. I felt like I was burning up. If I didn't get a hold of myself, it was going to be embarrassing.

Seventeen minutes later I was fully dressed, hair still wet, standing on her front porch. My phone buzzed right when I lifted my hand to hit the doorbell. My heart stuttered. For a moment I considered ignoring it and ringing the bell anyway. If she wanted to call it off, she could damn well say it to my face.

But no. I wasn't going to do that. I should. But I wouldn't. I peeked at my phone from the corner of my eye, like it was a snake that might bite me.

Taking a shower. Let yourself in.

Oh, thank God.

I turned the knob, half expecting it to be locked, in a cruel twist of irony. But it opened easily and I stepped inside.

And then stopped.

Christ. I hadn't stepped foot in this house in nearly a decade, but everything was exactly the same. Nostalgia hit me like Goat charging at my knees. The dark gray couch was the same one we had watched movies on every Friday night, each of us lying with our heads at opposite ends and our feet tangled together in the middle. There was the Tiffany lamp Emma had broken in sixth grade with a rogue volleyball spike and I had painstakingly glued back together. I wondered if she had ever come clean about that.

Beyond the living room was the dining room, and past that the kitchen. I knew it like the back of my hand. There was a time when I could have been sure that if I opened the fridge, I would find my favorite blueberry yogurt. Mrs. Andrews had always kept some on hand for me, since I spent so much time there. After she got sick, and Emma took over the grocery shopping, she had continued the tradition.

My chest ached. I doubted there would be blueberry yogurt in the fridge now. Emma preferred lemon.

I could hear the shower running upstairs, and I followed the sound. It was a large, rambling house from the Gilded Age, with three bedrooms on the second floor and four more on the third. I had no idea which room she had claimed for her own.

To my surprise, it was her old room. I wondered about that. Why hadn't she taken a bigger room, now that she had the house to herself? The third-floor bedrooms were the size of small suites, with large claw-footed bathtubs for soaking. When she was a child, her parents didn't like the idea of her being so far away from them. Then when she got to high school, she didn't want to be far from her mom, in case Mrs. Andrews needed her. But what was stopping her now?

She had left the door ajar and light spilled into the hallway. I poked my head in. "Emma?" I called over the noise of the shower.

"I'll be out in a minute," she hollered back. "You can wait in there."

I assumed "in there" meant her bedroom and not the attached bathroom. Too bad. I wouldn't have minded a second shower, not when it meant having Emma all silky wet.

I looked around. Like the downstairs, her bedroom was a time capsule to the past. Well, almost. The walls were the same pale blue I remembered, with the curtains a darker navy. The band posters were gone, as was the bulletin board where she had pinned pictures of her friends. Some of those pictures had made it into the frames that now topped her dresser. Not the ones of me, of course. Maybe she had burned those.

The bed, I realized suddenly. The bed was different. Bigger. I knew that for sure, because the feeling of being completely pressed against her, curling her tight into my body so she wouldn't fall off the bed, was seared into my soul. It had only been the one time, the night her mother died, but I would never forget it, the desperate need to take her pain and make it my own. The helplessness of knowing I never could.

I shook my head, trying to clear the memories. I did not come here to be sad. I was here to get laid, not reminisce about the past.

The sound of water abruptly stopped, and after a few agonizing moments Emma emerged, wet hair slicked back and a towel wrapped around her torso, obscuring the parts I most wanted to see but leaving plenty of bare, glistening skin above and below. Nostalgia fled. All that mattered was this moment, right now, with Emma standing mostly naked in front of me.

"Hey," she said. "Sorry you were waiting. I realized I was pretty dusty from digging through the storage closet at City Hall. You would not believe the stuff they have in there. Most of it's junk that needs to be tossed, but there are also these really cool old photographs that I thought we might want to display somewhere. Also—"

I could not care less about old photographs.

"Drop the towel, Ms. Andrews."

Chapter 21

Emma

Someday I was going to have a very serious talk with my body about the inappropriateness of its response to Eli calling me Ms. Andrews. When had something that had once annoyed me beyond reason suddenly become so erotic?

Probably around the same time he had told me he wasn't finished before putting his tongue between my thighs for the second time. Yep, that would do it.

"Ms. Andrews," he said again, more sternly this time.

I shivered even though heat was spreading through my veins like liquid fire. I wanted to drop the towel, drop to my knees, whatever he demanded.

But I also wanted to fight.

To push him.

To see which one of them would break first. And, good Lord, I hoped it would be me.

"Make me," I said.

His eyes flared at the challenge.

Every cell in my body went on high alert as he moved toward me with deliberate, measured steps. I tilted my chin in an attempt to look defiant, or at least unaffected, when in truth my pulse was skittering like a wild thing and my breathing had turned to shallow pants.

He stopped short of touching me. I couldn't breathe. *Agony*.

"I'm not going to take it from you, Emma."

I blinked. "No?"

He smiled slightly at my disappointed tone. "No."

It was all he said. The moment stretched and lengthened as we stood there separated by mere inches of air. I stared at the hollow of his throat, holding my breath, fighting the temptation to fidget. Was this his plan? To...to *awkward* me into dropping the towel? It might actually work.

Just when I thought I couldn't stand another second of this torture, finally—*finally*—he moved. I let out the breath I was holding in a shaky sigh.

He drew a single fingertip along the edge of the towel where it covered my breast, barely grazing my damp skin, leaving sparks of desire in his wake.

"Oh, no," he said softly, achingly.

My gaze shot to his face. "What?"

"Do you remember the summer I was a lifeguard? You had just turned fifteen."

I nodded. "I went to the pool every day with Suzie and Luke so we could all hang out together." It was my last carefree summer. By November, Mom's cancer had been discovered and my world had changed entirely.

"You wore a blue bikini."

"I had a lot of bikinis." It had been important that I look devastatingly cute, but I had never allowed myself to question why. It occurred to me now that it might not have been a generic desire. And it certainly wasn't about Luke. It might have been about Eli, specifically. Funny how I understood myself better now, looking back, than I had while actually experiencing it.

"Yeah, but that's the one I remember best. All your other bikinis had clasps like a bra, and I hadn't quite mastered bras yet," he said ruefully. "But the blue one tied around your neck in a bow and I knew how to undo knots. The first time I saw you in that bikini, you had your hair pulled up in some bun thing. I saw that bow and it wasn't even a double knot. All it would take was a quick tug and it would come undone. And I thought...*oh, no.*"

I tried to laugh, but it came out as a croak. "Why?" Such a stupid question. So needy.

"Because I knew that moment would change everything for me. I wasn't ready for it. Friends don't untie a friend's bikini top, and I wanted to untie yours like I wanted my next breath." His finger kept stroking, tracing the outline of my body, skimming from my wrist up my arm and shoulder to the juncture of my neck.

It was at once soothing and unbearably erotic.

"I wasn't wrong, you know," he said. "It did change everything. I tried to push it away, to ignore it. Sometimes I even tricked myself into believing it was nothing. I was a horny teenage boy. Of course I wanted to untie your bikini. It was completely normal and didn't have to mean anything. But then you would do something like, I don't know, smile, or be weirdly competent at something that had thrown the rest of us for a loop. Or stand there in a towel and say *make me*. And I'd be knocked on my ass again and think, *oh no.*" His finger paused at my jaw, where my pulse beat a rapid pace. "You wreck me, Emma."

I was melting, my bones turning to water. Fire and heat and a clash of wills I could handle, but this...this soft onslaught of tenderness dismantled my defenses with all the devastation of a summer sun melting the last spring snow.

He tilted my chin, forcing my gaze to his, giving me nowhere to hide. "Drop the towel, Emma. I want you to wreck me."

I dropped the towel.

It wasn't a choice so much as a need. Somehow his vulnerability had turned the power dynamic on its head. I was so entirely in his thrall that I would walk naked down Main Street if that's what he wanted me to do. Fortunately, he seemed intent on keeping me right where I was, all to himself, judging by the hungry look in his eyes.

He let out a low curse. My skin broke out in goose bumps—how was I cold and hot at the same time? He cupped my breast with one hand, his callused thumb scraping against my nipple until it was diamond-hard. The other hand snaked around my ribcage and pressed firmly between my shoulder blades. I submitted to his unspoken request, arching my back. I was rewarded when he dipped his head, caught my nipple with his mouth, and gave it a languid suck.

Oh, *God*. My head fell back on a moan, my hands digging into his shoulders for balance. His *clothed* shoulders. He was still wearing a black T-shirt, jeans...hell, even his shoes. Just like last time, he was fully clothed, and I was fully naked. Twice was not enough to constitute a pattern, but it was *something*. Like a childhood dare: *show me yours and I'll show you mine*. Or maybe he wanted to make absolutely certain I wasn't going to change my mind and leave the second he got his boots off.

It wasn't fair, and if there was one thing I craved, it was fairness. My life had been full of unfortunate events and terrible grief, but in this one thing, at least, I could have some control. I could reclaim my power. And if reclaiming my power also meant ripping his clothes off, climbing him like a tree, and rubbing my bare skin all over his, well, then so be it.

His shirt went first. I whisked it over his head before going straight for his belt buckle. He was silent as he kicked off his shoes and I slid his jeans down his legs. He stepped free and nudged the pile of clothes aside. Now he was every bit as naked as I was and *God*, he was a glorious sight. All that bronzed skin waiting to be licked. I wanted…I wanted…

I dropped to my knees.

Eli drew in a sharp breath as I wrapped one hand around the length of his hard cock. Slowly, I raised my gaze to his. I wanted to witness my effect on him. Wanted to imprint this image on his mind, of me on my knees, to remember for the rest of his life. Wanted to make him feel pleasure like he had never experienced before. Wanted to wreck him.

"Oh, no," I whispered.

And licked him root to tip before enveloping him in my warm, wet mouth, my gaze never leaving his.

His shouted curse was very gratifying. I tried not to smile, not wanting to lose suction even for a moment. I loved having him in my mouth. Loved the little moans that came when I flicked my tongue against the silky head of his cock, the way he hardened and thickened even more, the way I could feel his legs begin to tremble. I might be on my knees, but I had all the power.

And then the sharp, panicked tug on my hair when he realized how close to the edge I had driven him. "Wait—oh, *fuck*—not like this. Inside you."

I hesitated a moment, debating, then released him from my mouth with a long, slow suck that made him shudder. Suddenly I was swooping through the air as he scooped me from the ground like I was nothing. I wrapped my legs around his waist, locking them closed at the ankles. He took a step toward the bed and then stopped with a grimace.

"Condom," he muttered. "Hold on, honey."

I complied, gripping tighter with my thighs and throwing my arms around his neck. He held me with one arm and hinged at the waist so that we both dipped together. I laughed as he rifled through the pile of discarded clothes for the condom in his jeans pocket. Hanging slightly upside down, the blood rushing to my head, I took the opportunity to press kisses against the side of his throat.

He groaned. "You're killing me, Emma. Got it." He straightened, bringing us right side up again.

"I'll do it." I took the foil-wrapped square and ripped it open. "Don't drop me."

"Never."

It was just a word, meant only for this moment. It wasn't a promise for the future. I tried not to feel too much at the seriousness of his tone and instead concentrated on maneuvering my hands between us. By the time I finally rolled the condom down over his length, we were both breathing heavily.

Our gazes clashed and held. I shifted my hips, lifting up as much as I was able, and guided him to my entrance. "Now," I demanded.

His grip on my ass loosened just enough to let me fall on his dick with a slick glide.

"*Fuuuuuuckkkkkk*," he groaned.

I used his shoulders as leverage to lift myself and then slowly, achingly, lowered back down again. It felt so good that I did it again, and again, and again. Our breath came in mingled pants. I kept the pace slow, torturing us both with a pleasure that took us right to the edge of the cliff but couldn't send us flying.

I knew the moment he reached his breaking point. In a frenzy, he spun us around and tipped me backward over the bed. I landed with a soft thump and he was on me in an instant, pushing into me with such force that the bed moved across the floor. And, God, I *loved* it. My hips slammed up to meet his and I clawed at his shoulder blades. After the slow build, my body was now screaming for release.

Fortunately, Eli was ready to deliver. He hooked my knee with one hand and held me wide, so that he stroked my clit with every thrust. I was so close. *So close.* Then he swiveled his hips, grinding a circle against my clit, and I was done. Pleasure tore through me and I clung desperately to him as my climax wrung me out. I was still shivering through the last aftershocks of pleasure when he thrust hard, his muscles flexing under my hands, and shouted my name.

He collapsed on top of me, completely spent. For a moment neither of us could move as we worked to get our breath back. I drew soft, lazy circles along his spine with my fingertips and he made a sound of pure happiness. I nuzzled under his ear in response. I wanted to freeze time, to stay in this moment forever, feeling warm and sated and...

Oh, no.

I was wrecked.

Chapter 22

Eli

I opened my eyes to find Emma up on her elbows, staring at me with a sort of appalled fascination, as though I were a new and disgusting breed of insect that she was inexplicably attracted to.

"So," I said. "Pancakes?"

"Is that an offer or a demand? Because if it's a demand, then don't let the door hit you on the way out. But if it's an offer, then…maybe."

"I was thinking we could make them together."

Her head tilted, causing her hair to spill over her still-naked shoulder in a mussed curtain of gold. I twisted a lock of it around my index finger and examined it. She didn't stop me. It seemed like a small miracle that she didn't stop me. Even before the mess was made, when we had been the best of friends, I wouldn't have dared to touch her like this.

Of course, back then I wouldn't have woken up naked in her bed after a night that included two rounds of mind-bogglingly good sex, either.

I wouldn't go so far as to say the eight-year Emma drought was worth it, but my cock in her mouth and her hair twisted around my finger were certainly important points to consider.

"Pancakes sound amazing, especially since I don't recall ever getting around to dinner last night, but I probably shouldn't," she said.

I could hear the regret in her voice. She wasn't just trying to get rid of me nicely. Though, that could have been because she really wanted those pancakes.

I released her hair and it unspiraled from my finger like a pinwheel. "Why is that?"

"Oh, you know. That fun little thing called work?" She bumped her shoulder playfully against mine. Another small miracle. "What about you? Aren't you on duty today?"

"I have the day off."

"Oh," she said wistfully.

It wasn't my place to tell her how to run her life. We weren't friends. We were...well, it didn't matter what we were, because it still wasn't my place—

"Take the day off," I blurted, because apparently my brain wasn't in charge of my mouth anymore.

She gave a shocked laugh. "I can't take the day off."

I wasn't going to argue with her. She knew her own life better than I did. Except, of course I was.

"Why not?" I pushed back. "Does Cesar need you at the food truck?"

She shook her head. "Not today. He has his grandson helping him out. Marcus is taking my hours three days a week so I can get the bed and breakfast ready."

Her eyebrows pushed together, causing a worry line to form between them. I wanted to push my thumb there, erase her stress. I could guess her thoughts. Fewer hours worked meant fewer dollars earned.

She sighed. "So, no, I'm not making burritos today, but that doesn't mean I'm not working. I have the whole upstairs to paint."

I thought about that. There was no doubt in my mind that Emma was exhausted, mentally and physically, from having what amounted to three jobs, two of those full-time. And this wasn't anything new for her. In high school, it was school and taking care of her mom. In college it was school and waiting tables at Dreamer's Cafe. She probably hadn't had a day off—really and truly off, without care or worry—since she was fifteen.

She deserved a day to relax, and someday I was going to make sure she got it, come hell or high water. But today was not that day. Still, I could help.

"Okay," I said. "So we'll make pancakes and then we'll paint."

"We?" she echoed. "You're going to help me paint? It's four bedrooms, plus the hallway. Just so we're clear on what you're signing up for."

"I remember." I gave her bare hip a light smack. "Get dressed, Ms. Andrews. We have work to do."

"Why is that so hot?" she complained. She pushed back the covers and stood, apparently unconcerned with her nudity. I liked that, that she was comfortable enough with herself, and with me, to let me see her fully. "I'm supposed to hate it when you call me Ms. Andrews and boss me around. It shouldn't be hot."

I shrugged. "I'm only telling you what you want to hear." I watched her shimmy into a clean pair of underwear. "I might be giving the orders, but you're the one calling the shots. You're in control when it comes to me. You always have been."

She froze in the act of rifling through her dresser for clean clothes. Her eyes met mine in the mirror. For a fleeting moment, she looked lost. Fear skated across her features, there and gone again before I could fully understand it. She looked away.

"Or maybe it's Pavlovian," I suggested. "I've called you Ms. Andrews with my mouth between your legs enough that now you're trained. I say Ms. Andrews, and you get wet."

"Hey!" she yelled. "Did you just compare me to a *dog*?"

She grabbed a T-shirt from the drawer, twisted it, and whipped it at me, hitting me right in the gut. "I am not a dog, Eli. You can't train me."

She snapped the shirt at me again. I was laughing too hard to adequately defend myself, but it didn't hurt anyway.

"Are you sure about that? Let's find out." I dodged her next attack and, before she could try again, grabbed her wrists, holding her captive. I kept my grip light at first, then slowly tightened my hold, watching her reaction closely. Her eyes flared with heat. She liked it. *Interesting.* "Underwear off, Ms. Andrews."

I could feel her pulse pick up speed against my fingertips. She was turned on, but I knew she wasn't about to concede. Emma hated to lose.

She tilted her chin so she could meet my gaze, her eyebrows arched and her eyes gleaming with laughter. "Joke's on you," she said triumphantly. "I can't take off my underwear when you have my hands."

I laughed. "True."

I transferred both wrists to one hand, freeing my other hand. I traced the seam with my thumb. "Why don't I just check," I said. "For science."

With a giggle, she tore free from my grasp and spun away, out of my reach, sending me a teasing smirk over her shoulder. "You'll have to catch me first."

I lunged for her, laughing, but she evaded with a girlish shriek. And this...this wasn't a small miracle, that Emma Andrews was giggling and naked down to her underwear and most definitely wanting to be caught by me. It was a *huge* miracle, maybe the biggest miracle of my life. Although, my life was pretty short on miracles, so maybe that wasn't saying much. Still, it was big enough that my chest felt like it might explode from it.

I tackled her, rolling us both onto the bed. My hand skimmed beneath her underwear, seeking answers. I grinned. "You're wet, Ms. Andrews."

"Shut up and kiss me, Eli." She wound her arms around my neck, drawing me closer.

So I did.

Pancakes would have to wait.

Chapter 23

Emma

Maybe it was the pancakes, but I couldn't remember the last time I had felt so good. Peaceful. At one with the universe and all its inhabitants. We had opened the windows to keep the paint fumes to a minimum, and I could hear birdsong in the distance. I was *this close* to humming along.

I gave a happy sigh and stretched out the kinks in my back. Where had this sudden feeling of well-being come from? It must be the pancakes.

"You know what?" Eli said.

I looked at him. He stood with his hands on his hips, completely unaware that his posture emphasized the very nice muscles of his chest, and surveyed our work with a critical eye. A smudge of gray paint shimmered against his tanned cheek. My heart did a weird flip-flop thing in my chest.

It wasn't about the pancakes. It was never about the pancakes. The undeniable truth of it sent the room spinning around me. It was *him*.

"What?" I said, all casual-like, as though my entire world hadn't been flipped on its axis.

"You were right about this color. I thought it might be too dark, but it's actually pretty nice." He sounded surprised, but I didn't take it as an insult.

"Not me. It was Suzie's idea," I corrected. "But yeah, she wasn't wrong. She has a good eye for stuff like this."

Suzie had suggested a four seasons theme, with each bedroom decorated as winter, spring, summer, or autumn. We had just finished the first coat of paint in the winter room, a silvery, shimmery gray, the color of the sky before a snowstorm.

We had already done the spring room a pale green. Two rooms down, two to go. Plus the hallway. I hadn't forgotten that. If Eli was really going to offer his services on his day off, then I was really going to let him.

"When is the furniture coming?" he asked.

"Next week. I want the painting done by then and the bathrooms spruced up a bit. They're actually in really good shape, considering the claw-foot tubs are nearly half a century old. I'll wait until I have the beds put together and everything arranged the way I want it before I hang the art. Millie is going to loan me a few of her photographs, matching the theme of the room, so we'll have the Smokies and Hart Mountain in all the seasons. They'll be available for sale to our visitors. If no one buys them in six months, I'll buy them myself. But if they *are* bought, then Millie will send me replacements. Win-win."

"You're using the bed and breakfast to help the other businesses in Hart's Ridge," he said slowly. "That's brilliant."

"I mean, I'm helping myself, too. It's not one hundred percent altruistic. But, yeah. That's my plan."

I could feel his gaze on me, so I busied myself gathering up the brushes to clean so we could move on to the summer room. "That's why I was at Luke's the other day. I had this idea for gift baskets. One for each guest, full of coupons and samples and such. Luke is chipping in a coupon for ten percent off a meal at Goat's Tavern. Kate is donating a small bag of candy from Sweet Things. There's also a coupon in there for a discount on river tubing. All kinds of things—eep!"

My sentence ended on a squeak as I found myself snatched against his hard chest, his warm mouth on mine. He released me just as quickly and I blinked in befuddlement.

"What was that for?"

"I think you're awesome, that's what."

"You do?"

"Come on, Emma." His voice was gruff as he turned away from me, obscuring his expression, which I suddenly wanted to see more than anything. "You've always been my favorite. You know that."

"Your favorite what?" I couldn't resist asking.

He paused for so long that I started to think he wasn't going to answer. And then, at last—

"Everything," he said finally. "When we were kids, you were my favorite friend. When we got a little bit older, you were just my favorite person, period. Now you're my favorite lover. And I suppose when this is all over, you will be my favorite mistake."

Mistake. The word sat like a rock on my chest, stealing the air from my lungs. I couldn't breathe around it. Because in all those intervening years, I had only considered what he had done to me. The betrayal.

I had never considered what *I* had done to *him*.

Had never considered if maybe mine wasn't the only heart broken that night.

I had assumed that there were certain things friends didn't have to say out loud. Like, *don't arrest my dad*. But the truth was, I wouldn't have had to say that to Suzie or Luke. I wouldn't have had to say that to Cesar. Because Suzie, Luke, and Cesar didn't have the authority to arrest my dad, even if they wanted to.

But I hadn't told Suzie, Luke, or Cesar that my dad was cooking meth. I had told the one person who *did* have that authority. The one person who would need to hear those words.

And then I hadn't said them.

Good God, what an impossible situation I had put him in. On the one hand, doing his job and keeping me safe—keeping the whole community safe. On the other, arresting a man who had treated him like family and breaking my heart in the process. I could have made the decision for him, just by saying those words. He would have listened. He would have looked the other way, for me, if I had asked him to. Like he said, I was always in control when it came to us.

Why hadn't I asked him to?

Maybe because deep down, I hadn't wanted to. Maybe under all that love for my dad was fear and exhaustion. Exhaustion from taking care of other people's problems. Fear that there were no right answers. Maybe I hadn't wanted to bear the responsibility of such a horrible decision, so I had turned to the only person who could bear it for me.

The thought scorched my chest like heartburn. Acid rose in my throat.

Had I really wanted Eli to arrest my dad? Was that why I had gone to the one person who could?

After the first rush of grief, before the prison sentence had been handed down, I had felt the tiniest bit of relief. That it was over. That the man with the gun wouldn't be coming around anymore. That I was safe, that my dad was safe, too. The sentence had been a shock. Eight years. I had thought eighteen months, maybe. He wasn't a dealer.

Stupid. I was so fucking stupid.

Maybe if I had realized it was eight years, I would have said those damn words.

But I hadn't said them, and I had lost my dad and my best friend in one blow. And Eli…Eli had lost his best friend, too. He had lost me because I had shared something with him I had no business sharing, not without thinking through the repercussions.

The night he arrested my dad, he had waited for me in my home. I had screamed at him that I never wanted to see him again. And he had just nodded and left. Didn't even try to argue. No explanations. Like it was exactly what he had expected me to say.

I wasn't the only one who left things unsaid. Eli could have told me what he meant to do, but he hadn't. Just *don't worry, I'll take care of it*. In retrospect, maybe I ought to have understood that *I'll take care of it*, coming from a police officer, meant *I'll arrest him*. But I could honestly say that in that moment, I had believed he was going to have a talk with my dad. Like issue a stern warning. I had felt a little sliver of hope, that maybe if Dad knew the police were aware of his operations, that he would be forced to quit. If the man with the gun would have even let him quit.

What would my life be like now if that night had gone differently? Would Dad have avoided prison? Or would he be dead, too? I would never know, but it didn't matter. There was no use in dwelling on what might have been or wishing for if only. If only Mom hadn't died. If only Dad had made a different choice. If only I had used my words. If only Eli had used his.

If only, if only, if only.

That kind of thinking would eat me alive. I wouldn't indulge in it. If there was one thing I was good at, it was moving relentlessly, ruthlessly forward.

It didn't matter what might have been. The only thing that mattered was what was. Eli had betrayed me that night, but maybe...maybe I had betrayed him first.

It was a terrible, awful thing to realize that maybe I had wanted my dad arrested. That maybe a small part of me had hoped for it, so that at least one of my problems would go away. It was a hot iron pressing against my chest. I couldn't breathe around the weight of it.

I had never asked why he made that choice that night. *Why* hadn't mattered. Eli was a good man and he always had been. He hadn't betrayed me for money or personal gain. I knew that. And it had been easier to hate him for the role he had played than to face my own.

I had never asked him why he hadn't told me he was going to arrest my dad, why he hadn't given me an opportunity to stop him. To work it out another way. Why he hadn't demanded I tell him what to do.

Maybe I should have asked, then. And I should definitely ask now.

But I wasn't going to do that.

Because if I did, if I asked him why he hadn't said the hard part out loud, then he might return the favor. And I couldn't bear that. Even now, eight years later, I couldn't say the hard part out loud.

So I scooped up an armful of brushes and plastic sheeting and followed him to the next room.

What was one more betrayal, anyway?

Chapter 24

Emma

Everything was falling into place, if I ignored that Eli-shaped cloud looming in the peripheral corners of my mind, threatening to ruin my calm.

Yesterday's uncomfortable epiphany had changed the mood between us. I had tried to act like nothing had happened, like the word *mistake* hadn't triggered a come-to-Jesus moment in my soul. But I had never been very good at faking anything, and I could tell I hadn't succeeded yesterday, either. A few times I had caught him watching me with a question in his eyes. But he had never asked, letting me keep the pretense.

So I *would* keep the pretense. Eli was a problem that would work itself out when the election was over. He would be my ex-best friend who had betrayed me and ruined my dad's life. And I would be his favorite mistake.

My heart still burned a little at the thought.

But it would all be fine. Everything would go back to normal.

Except...except it couldn't, could it? Because normal, until a month ago, meant I hated Eli, and I didn't feel that way about him now. Not at all. It had been so easy then. So easy to hate him from up there on my high horse, judging him for his human frailties. Hate was a lot harder to pull off now that I understood how my own frailties had brought us both down in the muck.

And if I didn't hate him, where did that leave me? Where did that leave *us*?

Was I supposed to just *exist* in the same damn town as him, never being able to talk to him, to touch him, without all that steely hate driving me on? I didn't know if I could do that.

But I would have to.

I was flawed, for sure, but I was also pretty good at doing what I had to do.

Right now, doing what I had to do meant pushing thoughts of Eli aside and getting my job done.

"What's with that look on your face, Emma?" Suzie asked next to me. "Are you okay?"

"What look?" As if I didn't know.

It was a gorgeous summer day, the kind that brought a bone-deep sense of peace and gratitude. The sky was nothing but blue as far as the eye could see. Hart's Mountain was a deep emerald green, and beyond that were layers of blue ridges that lived up to their name. The Blue Ridge Mountains. I was so lucky to live here.

It was the perfect day for canvassing, as Suzie called it. I preferred to think of it as listening. The idea of going door-to-door, telling my neighbors who had known me since I was in diapers a list of reasons why I was a better than Eli for mayor, well...It was horrifying, that's what it was. It made me squirm. But I could listen to what *they* had to say. I could learn about their problems and help come up with solutions.

"It's a complicated look," Suzie said. "A little sad. A little annoyed. Kind of horny."

Kate and I stopped in our tracks and turned slowly to stare at her.

"Not going to lie, I'm a little disturbed by the implication that you know what Emma looks like when she's horny," Kate said.

"Fine. I don't know if Emma is horny. It's me, okay? *I'm* horny. And it's not fair," Suzie groused. "I spent the first three months spewing up everything I swallowed. I spent the next three months—the second trimester, where everything is supposed to feel great, mind you—I spent it with sciatica that hurt so bad I could barely go up the stairs. And now that I'm finally feeling good, I'm horny as hell."

"So, um, go have sex with that hot husband of yours?" I couldn't believe I even had to say the words out loud. This was Suzie's third pregnancy. Obviously she knew what sex was and how to get it. "Isn't that the point of marriage? Convenient sex?"

Suzie glared. "*Convenient?* Do you know how hard it is to find time for sex with two kids under the age of five, one of whom has suddenly realized he won't be the baby anymore and is extra clingy?" she hissed. "Do you?"

No, I did not. I sent a panicked look to Kate, who nodded.

"Hey, there. It's all going to be okay." Kate rubbed a soothing circle on Suzie's back. "Why don't you send the kids to me Friday night for a sleepover? Jessica and I would love that. Well," she reconsidered, "*I* would love that. But I'll pay Jessica thirty bucks, and she'll love the money."

Suzie's eyes widened. "Are you serious?" she whispered.

"Of course."

"Zack is still in diapers. I mean, you'd have to change them."

"I am familiar with the concept," Kate said drily. "I might have done that once or twice with Jessica, you know."

"Kate!" Suzie shrieked joyously. She grabbed her in a side hug, the only kind of hug she could manage with her expanding belly. "You're such a sweetheart."

I didn't think I was imagining the look of supreme annoyance that crossed Kate's face.

"Don't call me sweetheart," Kate muttered, proving me right. She gave Suzie a quick hug before disentangling herself. "You know I don't like it."

"I'm sorry. It's a hard habit to break. Everyone calls you that."

"You're going to hate hearing this, but it's because you *are* a sweetheart," I said. "You're the absolute best, Kate. Everyone loves you."

"Everyone loved George," Kate corrected. "*George* was the best. I'm just the girlfriend who got knocked up her senior year. People are only willing to overlook that because Jessica is all that's left of him."

"Having sex in high school is not a character flaw," I said. "Lots of people did it, including George, obviously. You're not even the only one who got pregnant."

"Right. And remind me how those girls were treated?"

I chewed my lip. Kate had a point there. I wouldn't say those other girls were shunned, exactly, but they weren't embraced with open arms like Kate. And that had nothing to do with Kate being more deserving, and everything to do with George. Hart's Ridge, like small towns all over the country, sent many of its young adults to the military. George was the only one who hadn't come home again. That made him a hero, in addition to being a good guy.

"It's just hard, dealing with all those expectations," Kate said softly. "Everyone wants me to be perfect for George, but I'm not perfect. And sometimes...sometimes I want to scream my head off."

My heart ached for my friend. "Kate..."

"It doesn't matter." Kate shook her head, her smile a little too bright. A little too brittle. She was done talking about it, and when Kate was done, she was *done*. "Let's go get some votes."

I exchanged a worried look with Suzie, who lifted her shoulders in an *I know, but what can we do?* gesture. We fell into step.

"So, where next?" I asked, because Suzie was the mastermind here. I was only tagging along because, well, I had to. It was about me, so I couldn't exactly sit this one out, no matter how much I wanted to.

My phone buzzed before Suzie could answer the question. I retrieved it from my purse, noted the unfamiliar number, and answered it anyway. Something I never would have done before becoming Acting Mayor. "Hello?"

"Ms. Andrews? This is Maria Lipscomb from the North Carolina State Historic Preservation Office. I received your email regarding the lamp posts of Hart's Ridge, and we have a problem."

I frowned. That wasn't what I wanted to hear at all. "Just a moment." I hit mute and looked at my friends. "I have to take this. I'm going to get a coffee at Wired. You guys want anything?"

They shook their heads. I unmuted the phone and darted across the street. "Sorry about that. What can I do for you?"

Ms. Lipscomb sighed heavily. "It's not about what you can do, unfortunately. It's about what you've already done."

That didn't sound good at all. My heart sank into my shoes. "What did I do?"

"The lamp posts on Main Street are registered on the National Register of Historic Places, which means that all repairs must be approved by the State Historic Preservation Office. You did not receive approval before commencing work." Ms. Lipscomb sighed again. "All of which is to say that you violated Section 106 of the National Historic Preservation Act."

My heart exited my shoes and sank beneath the sidewalk pavement. "I broke a *law*?" I squeaked.

"Yes. Yes, you did."

"Oh my God."

I sat down on the bench outside Hot and Wired and rubbed my forehead. My first official act as mayor broke the law. All I had wanted was to make my dad proud. To be like my mom and leave things better than I found them. That's it. A little thing, I had told myself. And I had failed spectacularly. Why had I ever thought I could do this?

"Okay. Okay," Maybe if I repeated it one more time, it would be true. Manifestation and shit. "Okay. What should I do? How do I fix this?"

"I don't know that it *can* be fixed, unfortunately. If the historic nature of the lamp posts has been destroyed, there will be fines. I'll need you to send me, in writing, everything you did to the lamp posts. The method you used for cleaning and painting. The brand and type of paint. All of that. Let's hope you didn't damage anything beyond repair."

"I'll do that today. Right now."

The moment I hung up, I started typing. Five minutes later I hit send. Now all I could do was wait.

I stood up, rubbing the stress from my aching neck, and looked up from my phone, searching for my friends. Instead of Suzie and Kate, I found myself eye-to-eye with Eli's new campaign poster. There was a picture of him in his police uniform, grinning his good-guy grin...and next to that was my dad's mug shot.

I froze, stunned. He could have walked up to me in the middle of Main Street and punched me in the face and it would have hurt less. It would have made me feel less exposed than I felt right now, staring at the photographic evidence of the second worst moment of my family's life.

Things were not falling into place. Not at all. Things were falling apart.

Fucking Eli.

Chapter 25

Eli

I was having a pretty good day until Mrs. Gaither, who was somewhere between the age of eighty-three and Methuselah, socked me on my shoulder with her purse.

"Hey, now!" I rubbed the spot where her bag had made contact. What the hell did she have in there, rocks? "What was that for?"

"Don't you play dumb with me, young man. I won't have it. Those posters are all over town. You should be ashamed of yourself." She smacked me again, on my other shoulder this time. "I'm disappointed in you, Eli."

That stung more than the clobbering. Mrs. Gaither had always liked me.

"What posters?" I asked. The only posters I knew of were the ones proclaiming my candidacy for mayor. She couldn't be pissed about that, could she? It didn't make any sense. "Honestly, I have no idea what you're talking about. I'm just here to get my coffee and maybe a donut. That's it."

Shrunken though she was, Mrs. Gaither still managed to grab hold of my ear and haul my face down to where she wanted it. "*Those* posters. Now, what do you have to say for yourself?"

I blinked, trying to get my eyes to focus on the image a mere two inches from my nose. The image blurred and then cleared. There I was, in my officer uniform...and there was Mr. Andrews, in his mugshot.

Oh, shit.

I pulled back, despite her grip on my ear, so I could see the whole thing. *The choice is yours. Do you want the man who puts criminals behind bars, or the criminal's daughter? Vote for Eli Carter. Vote for law and order.*

Double shit.

"What did that poor girl ever do to you to deserve this?" Mrs. Gaither demanded. She released my ear only so she could hit me again. "Hasn't she had enough sorrow in her life? No matter what her dad did or didn't do, she's done right her whole life. This isn't Washington, D.C., young man. This is Hart's Ridge, and we don't tolerate this sort of nastiness here."

"I don't...I didn't..." I flailed for words. How had this happened? Who had done this? Because it wasn't me.

Jacob Bronson. It had to be Jacob Bronson. Goddammit.

"There's Emma now. Maybe you can explain it to *her*."

I turned so fast I nearly gave myself whiplash. Our gazes clashed and held. And the *look* in hers. Oh, God. It damn near broke me. *Wounded*. Like a lover had stabbed her in the back. Which, fair enough. Only I hadn't, but she didn't know that.

She spun on her toes, hair whipping behind her, and broke into a run. She was literally running away from me. There was a time when I would have allowed it. Would have allowed her to leave me over a stupid misunderstanding, because oh well, she was bound to leave me sooner or later anyway. No point in making someone stay when they were determined to go.

But I had only just gotten her back. She couldn't go away so soon. Not like this.

Not this time, honey.

She had a head start, but that didn't matter. Emma wasn't a runner, whereas I put in three miles most days of the week. I caught up with her in a block, wrapped my arms around her like a lasso, and hauled her back against my chest.

She struggled against me. "Let go of me!"

"Just listen. Listen first, and if you still want to walk away after, fine. Just listen. Please."

She stopped struggling. Her shoulders vibrated, but I knew her well enough to know it was anger, not tears. She was pissed. That was fine. I could handle her anger. It was her other moods I didn't know what to do with—like how she had gone all withdrawn while we were painting. Something had been eating at her, but she hadn't seemed interested in sharing.

But her anger, yeah. She was more than happy to share that.

And I was more than happy to handle it.

I didn't know why that was, why all her fury only made me feel softer, and why that softness made me stronger. She was a wave crashing on the shore, and I was the sand, soothing the wave into placidity before it returned to the ocean. That was about the sappiest damn thought I had ever had, but so what? I was softer with her, and in that softness was more strength than I had ever known I possessed.

"Emma-bear." I leaned in, surrounding her with my body, and lowered my head to press my cheek against hers.

"You know I had nothing to do with this. You know that because you know me. Even the worst thing I ever did to you, it wasn't from spite. It wasn't like this."

She swallowed hard. "Everyone is staring."

"I don't fucking care."

I knew she didn't either, not really. She was used to people staring at her. At first with pity, because of her mom. And then with morbid fascination, like rubbernecking a car wreck, because of her dad. That hadn't lasted very long, because people had learned pretty quick that if they stared at Emma, then Emma might stare back, and no sane person wanted to be on the receiving end of a death glare from Emma. She had a way of making a person feel like they needed to get right with Jesus in a hurry.

"I hate that picture of my dad. Is that what everyone thinks of him? He gets out in less than six months. I know what he did was wrong, I get it. But he's not going to do that again, because it's not like my mom can resurrect herself and die of cancer all over again, you know? I want people to remember who he was before, all the good he did. He deserves a second chance."

"I know, honey. I'll take care of it. I have a pretty good idea who put them up, and I'll see to it that they're taken down."

"I'm trying to set up a life for him here, in Hart's Ridge. With me. The food truck, he wouldn't have been very good at that. It's a small space, just enough work for two. He wouldn't have fit. So the bed and breakfast…I don't believe in fate, but that's how it feels. Like it was meant to be. He would love telling people all about the history of the house and the town over breakfast. Seriously, he would *love* that. Everything was finally falling together, and now this? On top of…"

I heard the catch in her voice. "On top of what?"

"I—" She made a gulping noise that sounded suspiciously like swallowing a sob. "I made a mistake. The lamp posts…I knew they were on the historic register, but I didn't know I needed approval to fix the chipped paint. My first official act as mayor was to break the law. I screwed up, Eli. Like, really, *really* screwed up."

There was so much pain in her voice. I ached for her, for what she was feeling. "How were you supposed to know something like that? You couldn't have known."

"I *should* have known. There are laws for everything. It should have occurred to me that there was a law for this, too. My mom would have known. And my dad…well, at least when he broke the law he did it on purpose. If I had paid more attention in school, if I had learned what I was supposed to learn, this wouldn't have happened."

"Come on, Emma. You know that's not true. Not everything is learned in school. So you're not perfect. No one is. You're something even better than perfect."

"Oh, yeah? What's that?"

"There's not a word for it, because there's never been anyone like you. You have an incredible ability to make things better, not just for yourself, but for everyone around you. You're going to make this better, too. You're going to fix it. I don't even have to ask how because I know you're already on it. So stop putting the bar at perfect. You're never going to touch it, but that doesn't matter. You don't have to."

Her shoulders stopped vibrating and she leaned into me, just a little. "Okay," she said finally. "You can let go of me now."

I was disinclined to do that.

"What if I don't want to?" Not now, not ever. But I wasn't going to say that part out loud, because I already knew the answer. She wasn't going to keep me. When the election was over, we would be, too.

"I don't think you have a choice. You're in uniform, which means you have to work. You can't stand here on Main Street, holding me hostage all day. Unless you plan to arrest me. That's what you do, isn't it? Arrest otherwise upstanding citizens for their very first infraction?"

And there it was. I knew her nerves were frayed to their breaking point, finding out she broke the law while also seeing those damn posters. But she meant it just the same. She still hadn't forgiven me, not that I had ever asked her to.

And dammit, I was tired of it. Never mind that, as far as first infractions went, making *crystal fucking meth* was not exactly jaywalking.

I wasn't going to take this crap from her. She was sleeping with me, dammit. I had been *inside* of her. She needed to know what I stood for.

I released her and spun her around by the shoulders to face me. "Emma Louise Andrews, don't you ever say that to me again. I've made mistakes. I know I have. But I've worked damn hard to rectify those mistakes. There was a time, when I put on this uniform, I couldn't look myself in the face. I was too ashamed. But serve and protect—I learned what that meant. I learned how to do it, not just pay lip service. I wear this uniform with pride now. Don't you dare say otherwise."

She stared at me with wide gray eyes. I had surprised her. She hadn't expected me to push back, probably because pushing back wasn't something I usually did. Not when it came to her.

"Okay," she said, but I could tell she didn't understand. And I wanted her to. Wanted her to understand how I felt about his job. Wanted her to understand *me*.

"Come with me," I said impulsively.

Her eyes narrowed suspiciously. "Come with you where?"

"On patrol. Come with me."

"I was afraid that's what you meant. No, thank you."

"Riding along with a police officer, seeing that interaction with Hart's Ridge citizens, that seems like something a good mayor would be interested in doing."

She gave my chest a slight push. "That's a low blow, Officer Carter."

I noticed that she left her hand there, resting on my heart. I looked down at it, then at her face, my eyebrows raised.

"Yes," she snapped. "I like touching you. What of it?"

"Come with me, and you can keep doing that. Maybe I'll even let you hold my hand."

She rolled her eyes. "I'm not that kind of girl." She huffed a long-suffering sigh. "Fine, I'll come. But only because I want to be a good mayor."

I grinned. "Sure, that's why."

As I led her to my car, I grabbed her hand, lacing our fingers together. Because I knew exactly what kind of girl she was.

Chapter 26

Emma

I buckled myself into the last place on Earth I ever wanted to be. I had never been in any police car at all, much less Eli's. But I knew someone who had.

I sneaked a surreptitious glance over my shoulder to the back seat, trying to imagine my dad sitting there behind the partition, handcuffed and ashamed. It made my chest ache. I caught Eli's eye as I faced forward again.

"I didn't use the squad car to bring him in," Eli said.

"What?" Apparently I wasn't as subtle as I thought.

"You were thinking about your dad, right? He was never back there. After you told me, I waited for you to go to Dreamer's, and I took my truck. No handcuffs, either. I didn't want to give the neighbors something to talk about before I could see you again. I wanted you to hear it from me, not some nosy busybody who didn't love you."

I sucked in a sharp breath of air at the word *love*. He meant as friends. Back then, he had loved me, not as a sister, exactly, given what he had said about me in that bathing suit, but as a friend. The way I had loved him.

Although, come to think of it, *how* I had loved him was feeling increasingly murky. Having him back in my life made all those old memories come roaring back to the surface. Like how I had always managed to be single just in time for each and every school dance, so we could go together as "just friends." And all the little excuses I would find to touch him. I had always liked to touch him. That wasn't a recent development.

Anyway, this wasn't the time to think about that. This was about my dad. I exhaled slowly, trying to refocus my runaway brain. "And he just...went with you? It was that easy?"

"Well, sure." He sent me a surprised look. "He seemed almost relieved it was over, to be honest. Not that I think he wanted to go to jail, either. He said he had planned to get out of meth as soon as he made enough money. But then your mom died, and certain people weren't so keen on letting him leave. And then I caught on to everything before he could figure out what to do about that."

Only Eli hadn't caught on. His own daughter had. Guilt gnawed at my insides with sharp pointy teeth. Eli hadn't told my dad that part. His betrayal only went so far as necessary to keep me safe. He truly was a good man. And like he had said, it was a completely different thing from being merely nice.

"Thank you," I said quietly. And then hoped he wouldn't ask what I was thanking him for.

He didn't. He just nodded and put the car in drive.

"So where are we going?" I asked. "Do you have a place you're supposed to be, or...?"

"I start with patrolling 19E for speeders, then do a few check-ins in town. Things never really stick to that plan. I get calls, so most of it is played by ear."

"Oh. That's pretty ballsy of you, don't you think? Writing speeding tickets before an election? That won't exactly endear you to your voters."

"That...hadn't occurred to me."

He was watching the road, so I took the opportunity to study his profile. "It hadn't occurred to you, that people might not be so keen on voting for the man who wrote them a ticket? You do *want* to be mayor, don't you?"

"I want Hart's Ridge to have the mayor it deserves."

My eyes narrowed. That wasn't exactly an answer. "*I'm the mayor Hart's Ridge deserves.*"

He pulled his eyes away from the road long enough to flash me a grin. "Then I can't be too upset about it when you win, can I?"

"*If*, not when, and it's a pretty big if now with those posters all over town reminding people that I'm a felon's daughter."

"Once again, I had nothing to do with those posters. That being said, I don't think they had the intended effect." He rubbed his shoulder as we pulled into a trailhead parking lot to set up a speed trap. "Anyway, you also make damn good burritos, or so I hear, so there is that."

"This election is not going to come down to my cooking skills, Eli. Why aren't you taking this seriously?"

"You have to understand, when I threw my hat in the ring, there wasn't anybody else. Hell, the Whittakers couldn't find anyone even to act on a temporary basis. No one wanted it. Would you have been so eager for the position if I hadn't stepped up first?"

"Maybe," I said, even though I knew one hundred percent that I had only wanted this so he couldn't have it. That was how it started, anyway. Now things were different. I could be good at this. Really and truly good at this, and I could *do* good for other people.

It was funny to think how much had changed in the last six weeks. Had I really thought I couldn't live in Hart's Ridge if he were mayor? I felt so differently now. I wanted to win, absolutely, but I wasn't going to move if I lost. Hart's Ridge was my home, forever. And Eli...I didn't want to live far away from him. No matter what happened after the election.

"Don't lie to me, Ms. Andrews."

"Fine. Probably not," I admitted. "I didn't want you to win, okay? But what are you going to do if you *do* win? Mayor isn't a paid position, and you can't do it while serving as a police officer."

"*If* I win. I imagine the citizens of Hart's Ridge will take that issue into account when they cast their votes. A vote for me means losing their only full-time police officer, and possibly updating the law to make mayor a paid position. Unless they want their mayor to be homeless."

Realization dawned. "You jerk! You never had any intention of winning. You just wanted to trick me into it. You manipulated me. What an awful thing to do."

"Yeah. You should probably drop out of the race. Teach me a lesson," he said sarcastically.

I crossed my arms over my chest. "I'm not going to drop out. I want to be mayor. No, don't look all pleased with yourself. You tricked me. What you should have done was tell me straight out that I should be mayor, because I would do an awesome job."

"Right. And you would have immediately hustled your cute ass over to Town Hall to sign up, because you valued my opinion so highly."

He had a point there. My ass *was* cute.

And I wouldn't have taken his interference kindly, which was the more important point. But it wasn't like he had lied to me. I had made my own decision.

"It was a pretty risky move on your part," I said. "They might actually vote for you. You might be the next mayor of Hart's Ridge."

"Then I guess you better make sure that this Fourth of July is one hell of a success."

A white pickup truck zoomed past us at seventy-five miles per hour, twenty over the posted limit. Eli flipped his lights on and exited the parking lot. The truck pulled over almost immediately, and Eli stopped behind him. He ran the plates, leaving the lights still flashing.

"Wait here," he said, unbuckling.

I nodded. I watched Eli approach the vehicle right as another car went whizzing by, making Eli jump farther off the road. My heart leaped into my throat. I had known police work was sometimes dangerous, but it felt excruciatingly real now.

It felt like an eternity before the truck pulled back on the road and Eli returned to the car, but it was probably no more than ten minutes. I grabbed his face and kissed him hard on the mouth.

"What was that for?" he asked when we separated.

"I was scared for you."

His dark eyes warmed. "It was just a teenager going too fast, not a murderer on the run. I wasn't in any danger."

"You could have been hit by a car."

"Well, yeah." He buckled in. "That does happen, sometimes. It's one of the biggest hazards of this job. In a small town like this, we're more likely to die in a crash or get hit by a car as get shot."

"Be careful. Promise me, Eli."

He ran his thumb along my cheekbone. "I promise."

I sat back, my heart still beating a little too fast. "How much was the ticket for?"

"A buck twenty." Eli grinned. "His parents are going to be pissed, but maybe he'll think twice before he presses that gas pedal. I let him know this stretch is part of my regular patrol, so if he doesn't, I'll see him again. It's funny, because this is probably the number one thing people hate about what I do, but it's something I truly believe in. This highway is a killer. It's narrow and made of hairpin curves.

If I can stop one person from wrapping their car around a tree, I consider that a huge win."

I suspected his dad's death had a lot to do with that. I reached out impulsively and squeezed his thigh. He covered my hand with his, keeping me from retreating.

"I used to think this job was so easy, you know? Not that it's not hard work, but I thought it was work that was easy to do *right*. Simple. Everything was black-and-white. You break the law, I make sure you face the consequences. But it turned out that there's a lot more gray, even when it comes to the law. Maybe especially when it comes to the law. Justice is supposed to be blind, but I get the feeling that bitch peeks a little, and not in a helpful way. I realized that when your dad was sentenced."

Oh, no. I didn't want to talk about this. I tugged at my hand, but he held tight.

"Please, Emma. Let me say this. I need you to hear me. This isn't about you and me and what went wrong there. It's about me. How I do my job."

I swallowed hard and nodded. "Okay."

"You know what the cost of an inmate in North Carolina is? Thirty-three thousand dollars a year. For eight years, that's over a quarter million dollars. That's the cost to taxpayers for your dad's prison time for a crime he wouldn't ever have committed if that quarter million had been available to pay for your mom's cancer treatments instead. It's a fucked up system, and it put me in a dark place knowing that. Knowing I was a part of it."

He rubbed the back of my hand with his thumb. "I nearly quit the force. I signed up to do good, and it didn't feel very good to arrest your dad. Maybe I would have actually quit if Hart's Ridge hadn't gone in a different direction."

"You mean making a deal with the county to consolidate the police force?"

He nodded. "It was a financial decision, of course. It always comes down to money. Policing was the biggest line item of the Hart's Ridge budget by tens of thousands of dollars. And for what? Domestic disturbances, loose dogs, stupid conflicts between neighbors? I'm happy to take care of all those things—especially when the wife actually lets us make the arrest, which isn't often the case—but it doesn't make sense to have a whole police department ten deep to do it. We don't have much other violent crime here. There's been one murder in the last fifteen years, and the husband did it, open and shut case. Yeah, there's drugs, but most of that ends with charges of disorderly conduct. Hart's Ridge didn't need ten officers. We needed social workers and health clinics, not jail cells. So Hart's Ridge voted—you remember that."

I nodded. I hadn't paid too much attention, because paying attention to that would have meant paying attention to Eli, but I had voted, too.

"It turned out that what Hart's Ridge wanted was something I could live with. So I'm still here, and shit, Emma, this job is important. It kills me that you think it's not, that I'm just here to ruin someone's day."

Shame washed over me. "I don't think that. Really, I don't. What I said earlier, that was a terrible thing to say. I shouldn't have said it."

I caught his face gently with both hands, turned him to face me, and pressed my forehead against his. "I think you're amazing, Eli. Really and truly amazing."

Chapter 27

Eli

Amazing.

A compliment from Emma Andrews?

I hadn't expected that. Hadn't expected it, didn't know what to do with it, and was pretty sure I didn't even want it. They were nice words, the kind of words a lover should enjoy hearing, but to me it didn't sound loving. It sounded like the beginning of the end.

Which made sense, because that's exactly what it was. The election was only days away. Our time was almost up.

"Okay, then." I gently eased her hands from my jaw. "We should move to another spot. The kid probably told all his friends our location by now."

Her forehead creased in a frown. "Okay," she said slowly.

"Actually, maybe it would be better if I take you home."

"Take me home? Now? I thought I was staying with you the whole day. I think you were right. I didn't have any idea what it's like as a police officer, and a mayor should know more than that. At least have some understanding of what it's all about."

"Yeah. But I think you get it now. And I know you have a lot to do. I've taken up enough of your time."

"Right," she said uncertainly. "Well. Take me home, then, I guess."

I knew I was being a jerk, but I couldn't stop myself. Suddenly I couldn't get away from her fast enough. I needed some time alone, to think. Or not think. I would really rather *not* think right now, actually.

I turned the radio on and was relieved to hear Maren Morris belting out "My Church." A good song. A safe song. No star-crossed lovers here.

"You can listen to the radio while on duty?" Emma asked, sounding surprised.

"Sure. Police calls come through on their own speakers."

"Oh."

I hoped that would be the end of conversation, but I turned up the radio volume a little to make that clear. She didn't take the hint.

"Hey, did you ever find out what happened to your mom?"

I shot her an incredulous look. "You're really going to toss my mom out here with no warning? Jesus, Emma."

"Sorry. I've been wondering about it, but I didn't know how to bring it up. I figured this was as good a time as any."

She was wrong about that. It wasn't as good a time as any, though I couldn't put my finger on why that was, exactly. I felt out of sorts. Anxious. Like I could use a long run to nowhere in particular, so long as it was far away from Emma. The last thing I wanted to do was talk about my damn mother.

But I wasn't going to say any of that. I wasn't going make this a bigger deal than it was, because God knew Emma was going to make a big deal about it if I let her.

"Yeah. I found her. A couple years ago, I looked her up. I had her social security number, and she hadn't changed her name or anything, so it was easy. She hadn't changed her first name, I mean. She's out in California. Married. Two kids. Well, not kids anymore. The oldest is twenty-one. The younger one is nineteen."

"Twenty-one..." Her voice trailed off as she puzzled through the math. "That means she was pregnant when she left."

"Sure was. At least three months pregnant, unless he was a preemie."

It hadn't been hard to find their birthdates. Her social media accounts were shockingly open for a woman who had abandoned her family two decades ago. She sure didn't seem like a woman harboring a guilty conscience. But maybe she didn't feel guilty for those she left behind. Maybe she only felt relief.

I had thought about that final moment with my mom incessantly in the months after my discovery, reliving it over and over again in my mind. She had kissed my cheek, nearly lifted me off my feet in a hug, said *I love you*. I hadn't known then that "I love you" really meant "goodbye forever," and if her belly had protruded ever-so-slightly more than normal, I hadn't noticed that, either. But maybe I should have. Maybe there had always been signs that she intended to leave, and I had been blind to all of them.

It had gotten bad enough that I had sought therapy in Asheville, since mental health professionals didn't exist in Hart's Ridge. That had helped, somewhat. I had stopped blaming myself. I had always known, on a logical level, that a seven-year-old boy wasn't responsible for his parents' bad choices, but knowing something and feeling the truth of it was two different things. The therapist helped me *feel* it.

But that didn't change the fact that she had left me behind. I wasn't worth keeping, not to her. And if your own damn mother didn't think you were worth keeping, who the hell would?

"Did you talk to her?" Emma asked.

"There wasn't anything I needed to say. I found the records, flew out to California to be sure it was really her. I saw her. She got her mail, a neighbor said hello. It was definitely her. So then I spent a day at the beach, went to the zoo, and came home."

"You went to the zoo?"

"Sure. The San Diego Zoo. I heard it was worth checking out. The sea lions were pretty cool."

"I...okay." She seemed flabbergasted by this. "You made this trip by yourself?"

"I am an adult, Emma."

"I know that. I just meant..." She bit her lip. "I wish I had been there with you. For you."

"This was six years ago. You wouldn't have come with me. It doesn't matter. I handled it fine on my own."

"You shouldn't have had to."

But I had, because Emma had decided I wasn't someone she wanted in her life. She had that in common with my mom. It was on the tip of my tongue to say the words out loud, but if I did, she would make me talk more about that, too. And I really didn't want to.

"Why didn't you confront her?" she asked.

"What would be the point in that? She was alive. Healthy, from what I could tell. Happy. What was I supposed to do, force myself into her life when she had already made it clear she didn't want me? Hearing her say that wasn't going to make feel any better."

"But you have...brothers? Sisters?"

My chest tightened. "One of each."

"So you have two siblings out there, who might not even know you exist. Don't you want to know them?"

"You know what? I don't. I really, really don't. They're fine. They don't need anything from me. The only thing I could give them is information on their mother that they would probably rather not have. Why would I do that to them? They're innocent in all this."

"Because they would want to know. If I had siblings out there, I would want to know."

"Yeah, I don't think so."

I came to a stop at the end of the long driveway leading to her house. She unbuckled, opened the door. I was almost free when she pulled back.

"Are you coming over tonight after work?"

"Not tonight."

I didn't offer an explanation, even though I could tell she was waiting for one. Sensed her hurt and confusion when she realized I wasn't going to give it.

"All right," she said finally. "I'll be here if you change your mind."

I waited until she was in her house, the door closed behind her, before shifting into gear and hitting the gas.

Driving away had never felt so easy.

Chapter 28

Emma

I was so nervous I thought I might actually throw up. Today was the Fourth of July. If things went well, then tomorrow citizens of Hart's Ridge would likely cast their votes for me as their new mayor. If things went wrong, I'd be facing total defeat and humiliation.

Good times.

The first official guests of Holiday House, as I had christened the bed and breakfast, had arrived yesterday and immediately proclaimed everything charming, much to my relief. They loved the welcome baskets I had put together for them. I had sent them to Dreamer's Café for dinner, with a nice discount and a suggestion to try the lamb burgers, and showed them where they could rent bicycles to explore Main Street.

Not only that, but I had managed to get short blurbs in *Road Trip Magazine* and *Southern Magazine* about the Fourth of July event, and newspapers all over North Carolina had included it, as well. The budget was tight, but I had also booked radio and social media ads for a reasonable price. I suspected that our local celebration was going to have a lot of new faces this year—and hopefully those new faces would bring their wallets.

Adding to the good news, Hart's Ridge wouldn't be fined for the lamp posts. Ms. Lipscomb had come out to look everything over. I had provided photographs she had found that showed the lamp posts shortly after their construction. I had even bought similar flower baskets, which were now overflowing with festive red, white, and blue impatiens. Ms. Lipscomb had smiled at that, and determined that foreclosure had been avoided, whatever that meant.

Now it was seven a.m. and I was at the fairgrounds overseeing the setup for the day's festivities. Everything was going well. So well, in fact, that I was honestly suspicious that it was a trap and something catastrophic would blow up in my face, like an evening thunderstorm rolling in over the mountains after a bluebird morning.

I cast a steely-eyed look at Hart's Mountain. "Don't you fucking dare," I whispered.

"Who are we fighting now?"

I startled at the sound of Kate's voice. Where had she come from? Although I shouldn't be surprised she was already there, since Kate had a booth of her own to set up for the day's festivities. "Weather. Mountains. Fate. The universe. You know, the usual suspects."

"Oh, is that all. Sign me up. You know I'm always down to throw hands against the universe."

I snorted and bumped Kate with my hip. My gaze fell on Eli carrying rolls of lights to the barn and my eyes narrowed. He was already here? Interesting, since he hadn't bothered to say hello. "And maybe Eli Carter, too."

He hadn't changed his mind the other day, after he told me about his mom. I had waited up to see if he would, and when it became clear that he wouldn't, I had considered going to his place and having it out. But I had stopped myself, because that wouldn't have helped him. If he needed space, he could have it. It would have been nice if he had told me why, but he didn't owe me that. It wasn't like he was my boyfriend.

We had seen each other a few times since, quick moments where we talked about how busy we were before spinning off in different directions. Understandable, given that we were actually busy. Still. Something was off, I just didn't know what. I suspected it had something to do with his mother, but that didn't make a whole lot of sense, either, because he had started acting strange even before her name had come up.

And now he was avoiding me.

"Eli?" Kate repeated. She followed my gaze. "Ah. About that. Anything you want to tell me?"

I sighed. "I don't even know where to begin."

"How about with that time you made out with him on Main Street before he put you in his squad car? Start with that. Because the whole town is talking about it, but you haven't said a single word."

"We did not make out!" Which was true, but not the whole truth. "Not right then, anyway."

"Ah ha! I knew it!" Kate shouted.

"Shh!" I looked around, but Eli was far enough away that he couldn't overhear. "He's going to know we're talking about him."

"Tell me everything. Especially the sordid parts. Let me live vicariously through you."

My cheeks felt hot. Normally I was happy to share details, but somehow it felt different this time. The things that had happened between us were special. Intimate. I wanted to keep it all to myself. It was too precious to share.

"It was good," I said vaguely. "You know. Nice."

"Nice." Kate looked from me to Eli and back again. "No, I don't believe that for a second. I've seen the way he looks at you, and the way you look at him. The heat between you could start a forest fire in a rainstorm. No way was it *nice*."

I couldn't deny the truth of her statement. "It's...intense. But it doesn't matter. We made a deal. After the election, we're done."

"What? My God, Emma, why? Look at that man. I mean, *look* at him."

I looked. Eli was now on a ladder, stringing a garland of fairy lights above the barn door. No doubt about it, he was a gorgeous man. I wanted to touch him, because I always wanted that and I was beginning to think I always would. I wanted to wait for him to come down from that ladder and kiss him right there in front of everybody, like it wasn't a big deal.

I scowled. "You know our history. It just doesn't work between us."

"Really? Then explain all this." Kate spun in a circle, her arms spread wide, to indicate the fairgrounds around us, where everything was coming together perfectly. "Look at what you did together. It looks to me like things work between you just fine. What you mean is you can't forgive him."

For a moment, I considered agreeing with her. To take this confusing knot of thoughts and feelings twisted up inside me and boil it down to one simple concept: He had arrested my dad, and I couldn't forgive him. Simple. Easy.

But it wasn't true.

"I think maybe I can forgive him," I said slowly. "Maybe I already have. I just...I don't know how to live with it."

"What do you mean?" Kate asked.

"I mean..." I kicked at a tuft of grass with my sneaker and frowned. "I don't know what I mean. All I know is that two months ago, I could say with absolute certainty that I hated Eli Carter, and I could name my reasons why. Everything made sense then. Black and white, good versus evil. I wanted him to rue the day he decided to run for mayor. Remember when I said that?" I shook my head, almost in wonder. "I don't feel like that now."

"You don't feel like what, exactly? Oh, my God, you don't mean you actually want him to win this election, do you? Because I swear to God, Emma—"

"No. Hell no. Eli doesn't even want to win, anyway. I mean...I don't know. Things aren't so black and white. And they're not even gray, either, because that's just black and white mixed together. This is more than that. This is... You know how in kindergarten you would mix all the paint colors together until it was an ugly brown? That's what this is. It's all the pretty colors mixed into something ugly."

Kate tilted her head and studied me. "So, you're saying you don't want him to rue the day, then."

I allowed myself a tiny smile. "No, I don't want him to rue the day. I hope he has a very nice day, actually."

"Okay, you don't hate him anymore, you have very good sex, and he's handy with hanging fairy lights. What's the problem? Because I'm not following."

"The problem is that the better I feel about Eli, the worse I feel about myself. I feel awful, Kate. Like absolute shit." I scrubbed my hands over my face. "Because once I realized that everything wasn't black and white, that what Eli had done wasn't completely wrong, then I understood that what I had done wasn't all that right. Actually, it was probably worse, because I think I used my anger at Eli as a way to hide from my own actions. And I don't know how to live with that."

"Oh, honey." Kate pulled me into a hug. "It was eight years ago. You were barely an adult, and you had just lost your mom. Do you really want to carry this weight with you for the rest of your life? Let it go."

"How do I do that?"

"The same way you did it for Eli. The same way we do for anyone we love. You have to forgive yourself. You're not perfect. No one is."

That's what Eli had said, too. Why did everyone keep saying that? "I know that." I frowned. "Of course I know that."

"Do you?" Kate reached out, grabbed a lock of my hair, and gave it a teasing tug. "Because you look kind of annoyed about it."

"I *am* annoyed, Kate," I said crisply. "I was really hoping you would give me better advice. Because forgiving myself isn't going to make any of this any better, and if it's not better, then I can't feel good about myself, now can I. And I really like to feel good about myself, Kate."

Kate snorted. "Okay, then here's my advice. Fix it."

"Right. Now, how am I supposed to do that, again?"

"Generally I go with the same formula for every screw up. Apologies and acts of service."

"Oh." I blinked rapidly. "That's pretty good, actually."

"It is, isn't it? So you apologize to Eli for the eight-year freeze out and, I don't know, give him a blowjob and call it even." She paused. "And if that doesn't work—but I think it will—then you try something else. You'll think of something. You always do."

I took a deep breath. Apologies and acts of service. And if that failed, blowjobs. I could do that.

Just as soon as I located my courage.

Chapter 29

Eli

The event went off without a hitch, and I wasn't the least bit surprised. The Whittakers had been right when they said it practically ran itself. Hart's Ridge had been celebrating the Fourth of July with fireworks, a Ferris wheel, and a party for seventy-five years now. But this year was different.

For as long as I could remember, the celebration had gotten smaller with every year as the town contracted in on itself, with the older generations dying and the younger generations moving out. But this year was different.

Thanks to Emma, people all over North Carolina, and some from South Carolina, Tennessee, and Virginia, were discovering that Hart's Ridge was a place they liked to visit. And maybe, if one visit became another and another and another, the people who lived in Hart's Ridge could afford to stay.

That was the plan. And while it was too soon to tell whether it would really and truly work, it was a huge step in a better direction. I had faith. I had faith in Hart's Ridge. In Emma.

Who I had successfully avoided all day, until now, when dusk settled over the valley, and people were spreading out blankets and preparing for the fireworks to start.

"Hey." She shoved her hands in the front pockets of her jeans and bounced on her toes. "Busy day, huh?"

"Yeah. I think this is the first time I've stopped moving all day." I looked down at her, her eyes and hair luminous in the glow of the barn lights. So damn beautiful. My chest ached. "You did good, Ms. Andrews."

"So did you. I'm aware that I didn't pull this off entirely on my own, and I have you, the Whittakers, and dozens of Hart's Ridge businesses to thank for it." She touched the shiny blue ribbon pinned to my shirt. "And you won the pie contest. Of course you did. Did you save me a slice?" she asked hopefully.

I grinned. "I did better than that. I saved you a whole damn pie." I moved in closer, catching her by the wrists so

I could loop her arms around my neck. "But you have to come home with me to get it."

Her expression turned crestfallen. "I can't. I have to make sure my guests at the bed and breakfast have everything they need. How about you come home with me, and tomorrow we have pie?"

Tomorrow. The word sat like a brick in my stomach. I didn't want to think about tomorrow.

From inside the barn came a long glide of a bow over strings, signaling that the band was ready to play again. Jane Freeman, the lead singer for the Lady Killers, spoke into the microphone. "It's almost dark enough for fireworks, but I think we have time for one last dance. What do you think?" The statement was answered with stomps and whistles of agreement. "All right. Let's make it a slow one."

Without thinking, I grabbed Emma's hand and pulled her through the doorway and onto the sawdust dance floor. She gave a stunned laugh as I used our linked hands to spin her into my arms.

"Damn, Eli. You have moves." One hand settled on my shoulder, the other stayed clasped in mine. "What happened to the awkward shuffle from homecoming? I was counting on a repeat performance."

I laughed. "I can do that, if you really want."

"No." Her grip tightened, and I laughed again.

I had fantasized about this exact moment. Emma in a pair of jeans that showed off her delectable ass, dancing in my arms right there in front of everybody. Now it was actually happening and I didn't know what to do with that. I liked the way she felt in my arms, relaxed and easy, like it was the most natural thing in the world to dance together. I liked the way she looked at me, like she liked what she saw. Like she *wanted* to look at me. The moment wasn't even over yet, and I was already feeling nostalgic for it.

"I'm going to miss this," I said.

She looked at me in confusion. "You're going to miss what? Dancing?"

"I don't know. Working together. Making something big happen. All of it." Especially her.

"I'll tell you what. Next year, when I'm mayor, if you want to volunteer to help run this thing, I won't say no. In fact, what if...what if we just kept doing this? The mayor gets to choose their deputy. Why can't I choose you? The loophole that lets you be acting mayor when you can't be mayor—that means you wouldn't have to quit being an officer. Couldn't we do that?"

For a moment I let myself imagine it. Working together during the day—with a healthy amount of time apart to keep our sanity intact. Sleeping together at night. It seemed so logical the way Emma said it.

But it was a fantasy, that's all it was. Emma had a way of making fantasies seem doable and then actually *doing* them, but not this time. Reality would win, and the reality of our particular situation was that it was a fucking mess.

"This only works because we have an expiration date. We could mostly ignore our past so long as we didn't have to face a future. I don't want to go into work every day wondering if this is the day you're going to remember you hate me."

She stumbled slightly, and I slowed enough to allow her to regain the rhythm. But she stood there like a tree, staring up at me with gray eyes I knew better than my own.

"Eli—"

"Not tonight."

Tomorrow. The end was coming and I couldn't do anything about that. But by God, I was going to have this last night with her.

"Let's go," I said, heading for the exit, tugging her along with me.

"Before the fireworks?"

"Oh, there will be fireworks, honey. On that, you can trust me."

She huffed a laugh. "I trust you."

"Did you drive here?"

"Yeah. I brought the Airstream with Cesar. We made a killing on burritos today. But he has the key to the Tacoma, and he's already planning on driving it back tonight. I told him I would be finding my own way home."

"Presumptuous of you." But I liked that. We were on the same page. Tonight was for us, no one else.

I helped her into my truck, even though she was tall enough that she didn't need the assistance. I just wanted to keep my hands on her as long as possible. It felt like a thousand heartbeats until I got from her door to mine, slid into my seat, and put my hand on her thigh. She smiled at me in the darkness right as the first firework lit up the sky.

Between Emma's smile and the dazzling light display, there was no question in my mind which one I would rather look at.

And right now I was going to revel in her smile, the one I had somehow earned with a simple touch. I wasn't going to think about tomorrow, when she would no longer smile at me and I could no longer touch her. Those things were as inevitable as the sun rising over Hart Mountain, but that didn't mean I had to dwell on them. Tonight was enough. It had to be.

She needed to be at Holiday House, in case her guests needed something during the night and to make breakfast in the morning, so we headed in that direction. I focused on the feel of her warmth under my fingertips and the festive lamp posts on Main Street as we drove by. And this, too, was a moment I felt nostalgic for before it was even over. Sappy, but I didn't care.

I took her hand again as we walked up the path from the driveway to her door, releasing it only so she could bustle around and make sure everything was in order for her guests. The house was empty, so they were still at the fireworks, I reckoned, which gave us a little more privacy.

I took advantage of that by squatting low to drop a shoulder to her belly, then tossing her up in a fireman's hold. She gave a shocked shriek-laugh that made my heart nearly burst with pride. She hadn't laughed much during the last years of our friendship, not after her mom got sick, and now her laugh always sounded a little bit surprised, like she hadn't expected to be happy. I wanted to spend every day for the rest of my life making her laugh.

I carried her upstairs and deposited her on the bed with a bounce that made her giggle. Emma Andrews! The most non-giggly woman I knew! I toed off my shoes while simultaneously grabbing the hem of my T-shirt in an attempt to get naked as quickly as humanly possible. But she propped herself up on her elbows and watched me with avid interest, and I forced myself to slow down. Give her a show.

The shirt came off over my head and I made sure to flex my abs as it went. Her cheeks flushed a pretty pink. I liked that. When my hands dropped to my belt buckle, she licked her lips, and I *really* liked that. I moved a little faster after that, impatient, sliding my jeans and underwear down at the same time, in part because I was losing restraint, but also because if there was a sexy way to remove myself from my pants, I hadn't found it yet.

She didn't seem to agree, because the look in her eyes was downright hungry. I took a step toward her, but she stopped me.

"Don't move. I want to look at you."

I wasn't a bashful man, but it was a vulnerable thing to stand there bare-ass naked while Emma, fully clothed, perused me at her leisure. Usually I was the one in control. I insisted on it. But this was Emma, and she could have me any way she wanted me. God, I wanted to please her.

Our gazes collided and held. Without breaking eye contact, she peeled off her tank top, then reached around her back to unclasp her bra. Next went her jeans and panties, her gaze still never leaving mine, and apparently she did know the secret to getting out of her pants in a sexy way, because I was nearly salivating when she was done.

I hadn't moved from the spot where she told me to stay, despite that every cell in my body was vibrating for her. I waited, my muscles coiled like a lion who had sighted prey. Her hand slid across her belly and then, so damn slowly, farther down until her fingers disappeared in the honey-colored curls at the apex of her thighs, all the while her gaze stayed locked on mine.

I couldn't breathe for aching.

"I'm wet," she said.

That was it. I was done. Waiting any longer was impossible, as impossible as keeping my hands from filling themselves with her breasts and my lips from kissing hers. I grabbed a condom from her bedside table, tore open the packet, and rolled it over my length.

Her neck arched on a gasp as I entered her. I paused there, holding myself still, trying to get a check on this sudden overwhelming *need*. Christ. My chest felt like it was cracking open. No, not my chest, my entire being. Like the feeling inside was too much to be contained by things like bone and muscle. It shocked me with its enormity. What was I supposed to do with all this need?

"Eli?" She looked at me with a question in her eyes.

I couldn't answer. I was afraid of what the words might be.

Whatever she saw in my face made her own expression soften. "Eli," she said again, so sweet, and this time it wasn't a question. It was an answer. To everything.

I moved now, unable to hold back. Her nails dug into my shoulders, her legs locked around my hips. And now I knew what to do with all that need. Give it to Emma. Share it with her. Harder. Deeper. More.

She pressed her face against my neck, rained quick kisses there before scraping with her teeth, her internal muscles pulsing around me as she found her release. I was on the edge of my own orgasm, desperate now to slow it down, to give myself a little more time here inside her. A moment longer, just a moment.

But it was too late. Pleasure roared through me in a thundering wave, blindsiding me with ecstasy and breaking my damn heart. I held on tight to Emma, desperate to keep her close.

Just once more. For the last time.

Everything was for the last time.

Chapter 30

Emma

Pale golden sunlight shimmered through the crack in the curtains. I was already awake, had been for an hour, even though I no longer had to be up before dawn to serve burritos with Cesar. Old habits were hard to break, it turned out. Even when those habits made you miserable and cranky and served no purpose in your current life.

I rolled over. Eli was still asleep, his dark eyelashes fanned out across his tan cheek. He was so fucking beautiful. I could live with waking up before the sun rose if it meant waking up next to him. I could live with a lot of things, if it meant having Eli. Even my own mistakes.

It wouldn't be easy. I couldn't have a future with Eli if I was still keeping a secret in the past. My father might not hold a grudge against Eli, but a daughter's betrayal was on a whole other level. I didn't have Eli's excuse of just doing my job. I didn't have an excuse at all, except I was a mess. I had lost my mother and discovered my dad was a meth cooker all in the space of a month, and I had been messy with grief and loss.

There was little I hated more than a mess. Realizing the mess had been inside of me all along was painful.

Fortunately, I was good at cleaning up.

I didn't know whether Dad would understand why I had done what I had done. I barely understood it myself. He might not be quick to forgive. Hopefully he wouldn't follow in my footsteps and drag it out for eight long years. He would forgive me, eventually, but I hoped it would be sooner rather than later. I had faith. Love had a way of working it out.

Like I loved Eli.

Because, God. I did. I loved him. I loved him so much my chest felt tight, like all the love I felt for him was forcing my heart to grow bigger to accommodate it. It was uncomfortable, even a little painful. Growth usually was, I reckoned.

Footsteps on the stairs alerted me to the fact that at least one guest was awake and would probably want breakfast. I slipped out of bed, careful not to disturb Eli, and threw on clothes before heading down to the kitchen.

On the menu were blueberry pancakes, scrambled eggs, bacon, and a variety of fruits. Simple foods that were hard to screw up, because as Cesar had pointed out, while I was great at following instructions, a natural in the kitchen I was not. Still, everything was delicious and satisfying. Nearly everything was sourced locally, as close to Hart's Ridge as I could get, with the exception of ingredients like sugar and flour.

Selena, one of the guests, mumbled a sleepy good morning and tucked in, after taking the requisite photo of her heaping plate of food. It was an odd sensation, knowing that nearly a million people were going to see those pancakes, the pancakes I cooked. Not a bad sensation, just...odd. If all went well, some of those people would be booking their own stays here. I hoped so, anyway.

"Hey."

I turned at the sound of Eli's voice. "Hey." I waved the spatula at him. "Want some breakfast?"

"Wish I could. Everything looks great. But I've got to get going. I slept in later than I meant to."

"Oh."

He hadn't given me a morning kiss and, judging from the way he stood with his hands jammed in his pockets and six feet of empty space between us, he wasn't planning to remedy that. I knew he was feeling some kind of way about our agreement, and we needed to talk about that, but now was not the time. Not with my guests close by, eating pancakes.

But God, I wanted to kiss him. To touch him. To break down this wall he was building around himself, shutting me out. His words and tone were a shade too polite. There was no warmth, no intimacy. He might as well have been a one-night stand trying to make a quick exit.

"Come over tonight," I said. When he didn't say anything, I added, "So we can hear the election results together. You can bring the pie. Unless you want me to come to you?"

His eyebrows knit together in a frown. I had a feeling that, in his mind, we were already done. Over. Well, that was unacceptable. And I would tell him that, in no uncertain terms, but I was not going to do that in front of my guests, especially when Holiday House had only just opened for business.

"Please," I said. "Until the election is over, remember? The election isn't over yet."

"All right," he said after a long pause. "Six o'clock. I'll come to you."

"Six o'clock," I echoed.

He nodded. That was it. No hug. No kiss. No sign that we were anything but acquaintances. I hated watching him walk away from me, with this thing between us unresolved. Why was he so determined that our relationship had to end with the election?

My stomach rolled uneasily. Maybe the question had never been whether I could forgive him.

Maybe he couldn't forgive me.

Standing in a voting booth, my finger hovering over the box next to my name, was a surreal experience. I wanted to take a selfie to commemorate the moment, but that was illegal, and Eli would be pretty annoyed if I lost the election over something so dumb.

A trickle of sweat ran down my lower back. I was the right person for the job, wasn't I? Maybe the fact that I was even asking myself this question, and that I cared so much about the answer, meant that I was. Funny how I had barely paid attention to local elections, either voting for any old familiar name or not bothering to vote at all.

Now it was my name on the ballot and I was sweating over the choice.

Not that Eli was much of a choice, considering that he didn't really want it. He would kill me if I voted for him.

It wasn't even a paid position. Hart's Ridge needed to follow the kindergarten rule of "you get what you get and you don't get upset."

But I didn't want to be mediocre. I wanted to be great. Not perfect. I was never going to be perfect, and thanks to Eli, I was slowly getting more comfortable with that, little by little.

So, not perfect. But I could be great.

I checked the box next to my name.

From the voting booth I went straight to prison. I nearly turned around twice, but turning around would mean turning away from any kind of future with Eli, and that was unacceptable.

An hour later I was sitting across from Dad in the small visitors' room.

"What are you doing here, Emma?" he asked. "I'm always glad to see you, but I thought you would be spending the day shaking hands with voters, getting those last-minute undeciders, that sort of thing. Is everything okay?"

"Everything is good. Holiday House is already booked for most of the summer, so there will definitely be work for you to do when you get out next month." I couldn't believe it was really happening. Eight long years, and in three months it would all be over. He would be home.

If he still wanted to live with me after I told him the truth, that is.

"Dad, I have to tell you something. About that night. When you were arrested." I swallowed hard. My hands were shaking. I clasped them together and focused my attention there, unable to meet his eyes. "It was me. I told Eli you were making meth. It's my fault you were arrested."

The whole story came pouring out. How the smell—like a million cats had simultaneously peed in their kitchen—had woken me up several nights in a row. How I had noticed the empty packets of cold medicine, enough to supply all of Hart's Ridge, even though neither of us had had even a sniffle for several months. How I had put two and two together after randomly watching an old episode of *Breaking Bad*. How I had hoped was wrong, or that it was a one-time thing and he would come to his senses.

How that hope had been dashed when the man with the gun started hanging around.

"I was so scared, Dad. Not just for myself. I was scared for you. I had already lost Mom. I couldn't lose you, too. I told Eli everything. That's how he knew." I steeled my nerves and looked up. Dad looked as though someone had punched him in the stomach. "I'm so sorry, Dad. I don't know if you can forgive me. I hope you can."

"Oh, Emma, honey. What is there to forgive?" He scrubbed a hand over his ashen face. "I had no idea you knew. I had thought I could keep it away from you, somehow. That I could protect you. It made sense to me, that Eli would figure it all out. I always knew he would, eventually. He came around all the time to see you. He was a cop. This whole time, I thought I had put Eli in an impossible position. But he did what he had to do."

"He had to do his job. I think I can forgive that, but it's a lot harder to forgive myself."

Dad shook his head with a mirthless laugh. "All this talk about forgiveness. You, me, Eli—every single one of us was doing the best that we could. We all acted out of love. A little misguided, perhaps, but it was love, just the same."

He didn't understand. "Dad, I told a *police officer* you were cooking meth," I said, exasperated. "You were arrested because of me."

"Emma," he said, mimicking my tone, "I was *cooking meth*. Maybe you sped up my arrest, but I assure you it was always forthcoming. I might be a brilliant chemist, but a criminal mastermind I am not. You found the evidence because I wasn't any good at hiding it. I'm here"—he gestured to the prison around us—"because of my choices. Would I have made those choices if cancer treatments hadn't driven us to desperation? Of course not. But that's still not your doing."

I stared at him in disbelief. It couldn't be that easy. "So you forgive me?"

"You never turned your back on me. I betrayed your trust. I turned your home into a dangerous drug lab. And still, you show up here every other week. You loved me through it all. The question is, do *you* forgive me?"

"I never blamed you, Dad."

He grimaced. "You should, at least a little. A boy died from my meth. Just a couple years younger than you were at the time. I never told you that, but I think about it all the time. I didn't force him to take it. I didn't even sell it to him. But I made it, and he died. Even if you forgive me, I'm not sure I can ever forgive myself."

My eyes widened in horror. A kid died from my dad's meth? "Dad...my God."

"Your mistakes are nothing compared to mine. Let it all go, honey. Forgive yourself. You didn't kill anybody. All you did was tell your boyfriend to arrest me."

"He's not my boyfriend," I said reflexively. "And I didn't tell him to arrest you."

Dad gave me a speaking glance. "Maybe not in so many words. But you had to know what he would do. And not just because he's a cop and that was his job. He's Eli. He would do anything for you. You told him your dad was cooking meth and there was a guy with a gun hanging around? Come on. You knew he would keep you safe."

I closed my eyes. Of course I had. The thing I had pushed down so I wouldn't have to think about it. That moment, on the second worst day of my life. I had been so scared, my mind reeling with a thousand *what ifs*. What if Dad blew up our house with both of us in it? What if he was killed over a deal gone wrong? So I had gone to Eli, because I had known he would fix everything.

I had never let the thought form words. It was never a concrete hope, just a wispy feeling, like breath on a cold morning. *Eli would make it go away.* I hadn't even considered what would happen later. Hadn't realized that after an arrest would be eight long years of prison.

Hadn't realized that I would sever our friendship for just as long.

I buried my head in my hands. "I'm such a mess."

"We both are. I don't think you can watch someone you love die by inches and come away unscathed. Sometimes good people do bad things. Sometimes good people are a little bit messy. You *are* a good person, Emma. Your mom would be so proud of you."

"Dad." The word was broken, choked. "I'm not perfect."

"I know that, honey. We never expected you to be."

My face crumpled. "But see, I wish you *didn't* know that. I wish you thought I was perfect. You always knew I wasn't perfect because the one thing you and Mom wanted me to be was good at school, and I couldn't do that. I was such a disappointment to you, but I thought if I could be perfect at everything else, maybe you wouldn't mind so much."

I couldn't look at him. "When Mom was sick, I was a perfect nurse for her. I never forgot her medications, never cringed when I had to clean her up. No one cared so much about my grades, because of that. But after she died, I was such a mess. I wasn't the perfect daughter anymore. I couldn't tell you what I had done, that I had told a police officer you were cooking meth, because then you would *know* I wasn't perfect at anything. And I couldn't face that."

"Emma." He wiped at his eyes. "You're right. We were disappointed that you weren't a straight-A student and valedictorian and all that other stuff. It was what we expected from our child, because that's who *we* were. But, Emma, honey, that's *our* failing, not yours. We should never have put that expectation on you. There was never anything wrong with you. I am so grateful for everything you did for your mom, but I hate that we made you feel like you had to be perfect to make up for not getting A's. We weren't perfect parents, that much is clear. But, God, Emma, I love you, and so did your mom. Proud doesn't begin to describe how I feel about you."

"Even now?" I whispered.

"Especially now. Look at all you've done. Look at what you've built. And you did all that not because you're following in our footsteps with school, but because you're doing something you truly care about."

He didn't reach for my hands, because that would have broken the rules. But the look he gave me was as warm as a hug. "Mom would be proud of you, and proud of herself, too. She always said leave it better than you found it. And she did that, didn't she? Because she gave the world you."

Chapter 31

Eli

I had a feeling that hitting that little box next to Emma's name in the voting booth was going to be the easiest decision I made all day, and not just because Mrs. Gaither saw me walking up the path to Hart's Ridge Elementary School and took the opportunity to clobber me with her purse again.

It was because it was the right thing to do.

Making decisions was easy, as far as I was concerned. *Living* with those decisions was a lot harder. It didn't matter how long a person pondered something, unless they could see into the future there was no way of telling how that decision was going to work out. It was better to make the decision fast, and then get on with dealing with the consequences. Which meant I was fast to make a decision but slow to say it was the right one.

This time, I knew it was the right decision the same way I knew the sun would rise in the east and set in the west. Emma was the best for the job. That was just a fact. And she wanted to *do* the job, which I knew because she had told me so with her own mouth.

That was nice for a change. Not having to read her mind.

So, yes. Voting for Emma was the easiest decision I made all day. Simple, direct, black and white.

After that, things got a lot murkier.

Was it the right decision to ignore Emma's text at noon, asking if I wanted her to pick up burritos from Cesar or just order pizza for dinner, and ignore her again at three? Maybe. Then again, maybe not.

Was it the right decision to turn onto Emma's driveway at precisely six p.m., and then sit there where the asphalt turned to gravel until I was an hour past when she expected me? Possibly. Who was to say, really?

Murky.

She was standing on the front porch when I finally pulled up to her house, her keys in her hand. I was aware of her eyes on me, watching me put the truck in park, unbuckle, and slowly unfold myself from the driver's seat and approach.

I shoved my hands in my pockets. "Hey. Are you going somewhere?"

"To find you." Her eyes searched my face. "I was starting to worry."

"Sorry about that."

Except I wasn't sorry at all. Well, maybe a little bit. I hated to make her worry. She worried too much as it was, and I didn't want to add to that. But at the same time, I liked that she cared enough about me to be concerned for my whereabouts. I liked it a lot. And the thought of her coming to find me...well, it made my dick get ideas. I wasn't proud of that, but there it was. People only rarely came to find me. People were more likely to hide from me, come to think of it.

It was disconcerting to realize that my deepest kink might just be a very dirty game of hide-and-seek.

She nodded as though my apology was enough when I knew damn well it wasn't. Being an hour late was inexcusable. "I picked up a couple pizzas. It turns out my guests are super into this election and finding out if I'll be mayor. It's kind of sweet, really. They're all inside, watching the news for the results."

The words had barely left her lips when whoops and cheers erupted from inside the house.

We looked at each other.

"Congratulations, Mayor Andrews," I said softly.

"We don't know that."

I laughed. "They're not cheering for me."

Their phones buzzed at the same time, and at the same time they saw the results.

"It's official," I said. "You won."

She sat down on the step with a hard thunk. "I won." She stared dazedly into space. "I won. I don't believe it. How is that even possible?"

"The usual way, I'd imagine. More people voted for you than me."

She looked at me. "Do you think they made a mistake? Maybe they should do a recount."

I threw back my head with a roar of laughter. "Emma, you won. By a landslide. They called it before the polls closed. It wasn't even close. You have to accept that, honey."

Her jaw went slack. "A landslide? But...but *why*? People love you. You're the one who puts criminals behind bars and I'm just a criminal's daughter."

"Hey, now." I frowned. "You know I had nothing to do with that poster. But I have to admit, I think those posters actually helped you. People were furious that I would stoop so low. Old Mrs. Gaither hits me with her purse every time she sees me."

I smiled at the giggle-snort sound Emma made. "I'm not kidding. It was on sight with her. You have to understand, Emma, people love me, but they love you, too. They care. Your mom died. Your dad…well, he felt like his back was against a wall. He made a bad decision and that decision, yeah, it hurt people he didn't mean to hurt. But people aren't entirely unsympathetic to the situation that led him there."

"I see." She pressed her lips into a grim line. "They voted for me because they felt sorry for me."

I rolled my eyes. "No, you doofus. They voted for you because for the past two months, you busted your ass for this town, and this whole week was a testament to that. Hart's Ridge has never seen money pour in like this. Every business on Main Street made a killing, and it's because of *you*. You're the one who got Hart's Ridge mentioned in the travel magazines. You're the one who launched the social media campaign. You put this town on the map. People aren't dumb. They voted for you because they knew Emma Andrews would be the best mayor Hart's Ridge has ever seen."

"Oh." Her eyes looked suspiciously shiny. She blinked rapidly. "Oh my God."

"You're happy, right?" I knew she was, knew this was what she wanted, but I needed to hear her say it. Because it was ending now, and we had been here before. At the end of things. That had been ugly. I didn't want that. I wanted this time to be different. I wanted us to end on a good note instead of broken hearts.

"I'm happy," she said. "You know, my career choices have always been about survival. It's not how it was for you, how you always knew you wanted to be a police officer. I wasn't any good at waitressing. Delmy gave me that job out of pure pity. After that, I sort of fell into the food truck business because I had the truck and Cesar could make the food. Even now, with the B and B, it was just the best way to keep paying the mortgage. Everything I've done, it's just because that's what I could do with the resources at my disposal. I haven't hated any of it. There's been some good in every job I've had. But none of it was my passion. But being mayor felt *right*. You know?"

I nodded. "I know."

She grimaced. "It's just my luck that the career I'm passionate about is all work and no pay. But the B and B is booked up for rest of the summer. My dad will be out in a couple months, and he will help out a lot. I can make it work. I can do this. I *want* to do this."

I leaned back, crossed my arms over my chest. "Then you *will* do this. I would never bet against you, not when you're all in."

She grinned. "I have so many ideas. *So* many. Like an endowment fund. You know how fancy private colleges have donors that create funds for scholarships and things like that? Why couldn't we do something like that for Hart's Ridge, but instead of scholarships, zero percent interest business loans or stipends to do repairs on Main Street, and that sort of thing? We just have to find the right donors. I was thinking—"

She broke off suddenly and looked at me.

"What?" I asked. "You were thinking what?"

"I don't know." She looked around and then back at me. "I just…I love you, Eli."

Chapter 32

Emma

I hadn't meant to say it.

That was the thing about love. Once you realized you were in it, really and truly in it, you had to say it. The words were impossible to hold back. I might as well have tried to hold back the Chattanooga River as keep those words from reaching Eli's ears.

It was a relief to finally set those words free. I should have said it eight years ago. I should have said a lot of things eight years ago. Maybe all those things were tied together somehow, and now that I had said part of it, I could finally say the rest.

And that was a relief, too. That I was finally coming clean after eight years of swimming through murkiness.

I suspected the relief was all mine, though, because Eli was looking at me with something like horror on his face. He still hadn't said anything.

So I figured I might as well keep going.

"I love you," I repeated. "I think maybe I've always loved you, but I didn't always know what to do with that. Now I do. I need to apologize. I'm so sorry, Eli."

His brow furrowed. "For what? What could you possibly have to feel sorry for?"

He didn't say anything about the other part, I noticed. The part about me loving him. That didn't feel great. But okay. So we weren't going to have one of those magical moments like in the movies where those three little words could fix everything, and we would say them and melt into each other's arms and screw our brains out.

We could still have that moment, just not now. Now we would have to put in the work to earn it.

I could do that. I *would* do that.

"I'm sorry because eight years ago, something terrible happened, and I let you take the blame for all of it. For your part. For my dad's." I swallowed hard. "For mine."

He took a step back, shaking his head. "You don't have to do this. It was a long time ago."

"I do have to do this. I want to do this, because I want to be with you, and that's never going to happen if we don't put the past to rest."

"Emma—"

"Please let me. Then you can say whatever it is you need to say." I had a pretty good idea that I wasn't going to like it, but I would hear him out. And then I would tell him how wrong he was. Because this thing with us, it could work. I knew it could. There was too much love for it not to work.

He nodded. "Okay."

"It wasn't fair, making it all your fault. I don't have an excuse. I was a mess. I still am pretty messy, but I'm working to sort myself out now. I saw my dad today. And I told him...I told him about that night. I told him it was me. I was the one who told the police he had been cooking meth."

"You told your best friend," he corrected.

"Who happened to be a cop." I grimaced. "I wasn't unaware of your job, Eli. I knew what an awful position I was putting you in. I just refused to think about it. And then after...I kept on refusing. Because if I thought about it, then I might realize that I didn't just hate you. I hated my dad. I hated myself. It didn't occur to me that I didn't have to hate anybody. That just because I was mad didn't mean I had to stay mad for eight years. I didn't have to carry all that anger inside me. I could have set that burden down and walked away from it." I looked at him and my heart ached. I wished he wouldn't stand so far away. "I should have."

He leaned against the porch column, chin tucked low, eyes on the ground. *Look at me, please,* I begged silently. *Give me some indication that you understand.*

But he didn't, and I plowed forward anyway. "I wanted so badly to be the perfect daughter. The daughter my dad wanted. The daughter my mother deserved. And I...I couldn't face how spectacularly I had screwed up. At the time, I could see only one way forward: you. Now, of course, I want to kick myself. Why didn't I go directly to my dad and tell him to stop? Why didn't I at least try?"

"Emma, you—" He blew out a long breath and shook his head. "That might have worked, or it might not have. He might have stopped and maybe that would have gotten him killed. You don't know. We can't possibly know. But I do know that your dad loves you. None of us are perfect."

"That's what he said too, when I told him."

"Well, there you go, then."

I cocked my head. "Does that mean you forgive me?"

"There's nothing to forgive."

"Fine. Does that mean you accept my apology, then?"

"Emma." He looked at me, finally. "Of course I do."

"Good. Because I love you."

His expression changed, and I didn't like it one bit. He didn't look like a man who had just heard *I love you* and was going to say it back. No, he looked like a man gearing up to lecture a child on The Way Things Worked in the Real World.

"We had a deal," he said kindly. Condescendingly. "Until the election, that's it."

I gritted my teeth. Of course he wasn't going to make this easy. Because he was as big a coward as I was, only he hadn't faced that yet.

"The deal was bullshit. You know that. I know that. It's a stupid excuse. I don't care that we made some agreement, because that's what we had to tell ourselves to allow us to do what we wanted to do. It was fake. I'm over pretending things to myself, the good and the bad. I love you, and I want to be with you."

"Right *now* you want to be with me. You only just now decided to heal a wound that's been festering for eight years. What makes you think tomorrow it won't open up again? What makes you think that tomorrow you won't hate me?"

"Because I love you." My eyes burned, and I blinked rapidly. Dammit, I wasn't going to cry. "Because you could stack all the hate I felt in those eight years and it wouldn't hold a candle to all the love I feel for you in one millisecond. It's a love worth facing my demons for. I would face a million more, if it meant being with you."

"I don't feel that way."

All the breath left me in a gasp, like he had punched me in the chest. "You don't...you don't love me?"

His jaw shifted and clenched, and I could tell he was struggling to find the right words. He never lied, but that didn't mean he was completely honest. He had always said what I needed to hear. And when what I needed to hear wasn't exactly the truth, he left a lot more unsaid.

What was he going to leave unsaid now? Because whatever next came out of his mouth, it wasn't going to be the whole truth.

"There are lots of ways of loving, and of course I feel some of those ways for you," he said. "But this...what you're asking for...that's not what this is. It's not what *we* are. I can't do this with you."

"With me," I repeated. So specific. My heart cracked open. I couldn't breathe for pain.

"It's better this way. You'll see."

I stood there, frozen, as he turned away and walked down the steps. Kept going down the sidewalk, farther away from me with each step, until he got into his truck.

I kept thinking he would stop, that he would come back, that he would realize this was a mistake somehow.

But he didn't. He drove away instead.

Grief poured through me. I was familiar with the feeling, but that was no comfort. I was tired of grieving the people I loved. Mom. Dad. Eli.

It wasn't better this way.

I didn't see how it could ever be better again.

Chapter 33

Eli

Everything was fine.

It was Wednesday, which meant I had my usual patrol of 19E, followed by a long, slow drive from one end of Hart's Ridge to the other. It didn't matter that this particular Wednesday was the day after the election, and it definitely didn't matter that Emma had left me for the last time yesterday. There was work to be done, and so I did it.

Because everything was fine.

Usually when that work was done, I stopped by Goat's Tavern to hang out with Luke for a couple hours, but tonight I headed straight home. Luke had a way of pulling information out of a person, whether that person wanted to share the information or not, and I wasn't in the mood for that. Not that there was anything to share, anyway.

Because everything was fine.

I set the oven to preheat, grabbed a frozen pizza from the freezer, and put it on the counter. But I didn't want frozen pizza. I wanted pasta that was too chewy in some places, and too hard in others. I wanted cheese that was burned around the edges. The pizza went back in the freezer, and out came the lasagna.

Frozen lasagna wasn't much better than frozen pizza. But it had been my favorite of all the frozen dinners growing up. It was more expensive than pizza or potpie, so it was a rare treat. It also took twice as long to cook as a frozen pizza, which had meant something in and of itself to me as a kid. If I smelled lasagna when I walked in the door, I knew my dad was sober. And if Dad was sober, then everything was fine.

Right now, I really needed everything to be fine. I just had to redefine the word, that was all. Fine now meant every layer of my skin had been scraped off. Because that was how I felt. Raw and bloody and...and exposed.

That was fine.

The lasagna went in the oven. I cracked open a soda and flopped onto my recliner to wait. An hour later, I pulled it from the oven, piping hot and oozing nostalgic goodness, just as the doorbell rang. My heart gave a pitiful throb of hope.

I told myself it wasn't her as I crossed the kitchen into the living room. People who left didn't come back. I knew that. Clearly the message hadn't gotten through to my heart though, because when I opened the door and saw who was on the other side, it felt like it cracked in two.

It wasn't her.

"Hey, man. Do I smell lasagna?" Luke pushed past me through the door. "I could eat."

I followed him into the kitchen. "What are you doing here?"

"Checking on you. Where are your forks?"

I sighed. I produced two forks from a drawer and handed one to Luke. "I'm fine." I gestured to the lasagna on the counter between us. "Help yourself."

Luke sectioned off a good-sized chunk with his fork and shoveled it into his mouth. He gave me a once-over while he chewed, then swallowed and shook his head. "You're not fine. If you were fine, you would have stopped by the bar after work. Or you would be with Emma."

I winced. Because the hot cheese burned the roof of my mouth. Not because it hurt to hear her name. "I didn't feel like going out tonight. This might come as a shock to you, but some of us aren't scared to spend even a single second alone. Some of us even like it."

"We're not talking about my issues tonight. We're talking about yours."

"I don't have issues."

Luke snorted. "Oh, you most definitely have issues. If you didn't, you would be sharing this lasagna with Emma right now, not me, and you probably wouldn't look like I punched you in the gut every time I say her name."

"You can say any name you want. I don't care," I lied.

"Really?" Luke wiped his mouth with a napkin. "Emma, Emma, Emma," he said in a singsong voice.

Each time hit me in the chest, not in the gut, which proved Luke was wrong.

"You're an asshole," I muttered.

"I know."

"Listen, I appreciate you coming by, but there's nothing to talk about. We agreed this thing with us would end with the election. The election is over, so we're done, and she left. How did you even know about it, anyway?"

"That depends on what you mean by *it*. I knew there was something between you when you ordered her out of my bar. I knew you had messed it up when Suzie paid me a visit today and told me all about it."

"Suzie?" I tried not to look too eager. "What did she say?"

"I just told you."

I gritted my teeth in frustration. "I mean—"

"I know what you mean, man." Luke grinned and pointed at me with his fork. "You want details. You want to know if Emma is eating her feelings with a giant pan of lasagna."

I looked down at the half-eaten pan of lasagna, then back at Luke. "That's not what I'm doing."

"Right." Luke helped himself to two beers from the fridge, which was fair enough, I supposed, since I had gotten more free drinks than I could count from Goat's Tavern over the years. He popped the top of both and handed one to me. "You can drink this, right? Without violating your own rules, I mean. Since you're not sad."

I rubbed the back of my neck. I wanted it. It would feel damn good right about now, especially if I chased that beer with a bottle of whiskey. "I'm sticking with soda tonight."

"Right." Luke smirked. "Anyway, Emma is doing about the same as you, I hear. I don't know about the lasagna, but Suzie said she cried."

"Oh." Why didn't that make me feel better? I took a long swallow of soda. That didn't make me feel better, either.

Luke lifted his beer in a salute. "Two months. That's a record for you, isn't it? Emma sure had you running scared."

Scared? I wasn't scared.

"I told you," I said, annoyed. "We had a deal."

"And I'm telling you, that's bullshit. Who cares if you agreed to end things after the election? That was dumb. You're in love with her. You have always been in love with her. You made that deal because you were scared of getting hurt. And now look where you're at. Hurt. So go tell her you were dumb and get on with being happy."

As if it were that simple.

"You don't get it. She left—"

Luke tilted his head. "You keep saying that. But she didn't leave. *You* left. You broke up with her. Left her standing on her porch. What was she supposed to do, follow you and drag you back?"

Yes. "No, I mean—" Hell, what *did* I mean? I pinched the bridge of my nose. A kiss on the cheek, *I love you*, dark hair tickling my ear. No, wait, that was my mom. Hands clenched into fists, *I never want to see you again*. That was Emma...not yesterday, but it was still her. "She didn't talk to me for eight years. Eight *years*. What am I supposed to do with that?"

Luke shrugged.

"No, seriously. Tell me what I'm supposed to do." I was angry now. "That's why you're here, isn't it? You have all the answers. So go ahead. Tell me how I'm letting a childhood trauma ruin all my relationships. Tell me that I'm so scared of getting hurt that I bail before they can. Tell me I'm just repeating that same old pattern with Emma. Go on."

Luke leaned against the counter. "If you already know all that, there doesn't seem to be much point in me saying it."

"It's different with Emma. I was already in love with her when we started this, you were right about that. How could I end things before I had feelings when the feelings were already there? And I couldn't leave before she left me because she had already done that too, eight years ago. Who's to say she wouldn't do that again? If I hadn't broken things off. If...if we got married, had babies." *Christ.* The thought of it made me ache with longing. I shook my head and soldiered through. "And then I do something to piss her off, or maybe she's just had enough. Whatever. So she leaves. I couldn't take that."

Luke looked at me.

I held up my hand. "I know what you're going to say. Emma isn't my mom. She doesn't have some secret family stashed somewhere. She's not going to leave me just because my mom did."

"I wasn't going to say that."

That was disappointing. A small part of me had hoped Luke might actually be able to talk some sense into me, to make it okay to be with Emma. "You weren't?"

"No." He swallowed another mouthful of lasagna. "Personally, I don't think Emma has the temperament to pull off a secret family, so you're probably safe there. And, yeah, she's grown up a bit since she was twenty, and you're not planning to arrest her dad any time soon. But she left you once and maybe she'll do it again. I'm not going to stand here and tell you otherwise, because how the hell would I know? But I do know this." Luke braced his hands on the countertop and leaned in. "You're not your dad."

I blinked. "What?"

"You're not your dad. You're not going to numb your feelings with alcohol and waste your life not really living it. You're going to hurt, and eat lasagna, and then get on with being alive. Sure, there will be scars, and trust won't come as easy. But you would get through it. Hell, you'd even be happy sometimes. And if you did have a kid, you sure as hell wouldn't let him fend for himself with frozen dinners so you could get drunk and stay drunk. Because you're not your dad. I know this because you didn't fall apart when your mom left, and you didn't fall apart when everything blew up with Emma eight years ago. You were a mess for a while there, sure. But you pulled through."

A lightning bolt on a clear summer day would have surprised me less than Luke Buchanan delivering an epiphany over a pan of lasagna.

It wasn't about my mom.

It had never been about my mom. Not really.

I wasn't scared of Emma becoming my mother. I was scared of becoming my dad. I was scared of living a half-life, of retreating into a whiskey bottle to numb the pain. I was scared that I wouldn't have the fortitude to recover from a broken heart.

All those other relationships, before Emma. They were safe. I had purposefully chosen women who wouldn't hurt me because they couldn't. Nice women, fun women, but not a damn one of them lit a fire in me the way Emma did. But even so, I hadn't stuck around long enough to give any of them a real chance.

That hadn't worked with Emma. I was already in too deep by the time we had struck our deal. She had hurt me once, and she would do it again, I was sure of it. Agreeing on an end date, that was just my way of setting the parameters of the pain she would inflict when she left. The deal had been a wall around my heart. How bad could she hurt me when I knew the end was inevitable?

A hell of a lot, it turned out. Because I had known it was coming, had fucking *guaranteed* it, but it still hurt. It still felt like I had swallowed an entire black hole and it was now taking up residence in my stomach, slowly sucking all my organs into the abyss.

I wasn't going to get drunk tonight to try to mitigate that. The next beer I had, whenever that might be, it wasn't going to send me into a spiral of drunkenness. I knew that for damn sure.

Slowly I raised my eyes to meet Luke's. "I'm not my dad."

"No, you're not. So stop being such a damn coward and go fix things with Emma. Oh, hey, look at that." Luke grinned widely, clearly pleased with himself. "It turns out I *do* have the all the answers, after all."

I resisted the urge to bean the empty bottle of beer at Luke's head. "One day, it's going to be you sobbing into your lasagna, and I'm going to be the one with pithy advice."

"I don't know what pithy means, but I can guarantee you the sobbing part will never happen."

I was petty enough that I hoped otherwise, but I wasn't going to argue. It didn't matter. The only thing that mattered was Emma. I was ready to give this a chance, not just sex with an end date, not just a couple months. I was all in.

But I had the feeling I was going to have a hell of a time convincing her of that.

Chapter 34

Emma

I stared at the ceiling fan and thought. The guests had left that morning, which was a relief, because I didn't want them to think their innkeeper was insane. That wouldn't be good for business. My next guests wouldn't arrive until Friday. Until then, I was free to stare at the ceiling fan and ponder the mysteries of life in general and Eli Carter in particular.

I had spent most of the day curled up in a ball crying. Cesar had come by to drop off some paperwork and found me like that. He stayed only long enough to figure out it was boy trouble before calling in Kate and Suzie to handle it. Kate had called Eli every name in the book, but Suzie had staunchly refused to on the grounds that everything would be fine within a week, and she didn't want to have that on her conscience when we were friends again.

Her optimism was very Suzie-like and annoying as hell.

It didn't take a psychologist to know that Eli had issues. Not commitment issues. Eli was the most committed man I knew. To his job, to this town, to his friends. Everything he did, he committed one hundred percent of himself. No, what Eli had was a deep and abiding fear of being left.

And maybe his mother had started it, but I had pretty well finished it. I couldn't deny that. It sucked. It seemed that every time I thought I had a handle on getting myself sorted, I found another way I had fallen short. Freezing out my best friend with abandonment issues for eight years was a pretty long way to fall.

But I could pull myself up again. I was getting really good at that. The thing about facing my imperfections was that it seemed to go hand-in-hand with discovering new strengths.

There were lots of ways of loving, he had said. Maybe he was telling the whole truth, and he only loved me like a friend. Or maybe that was only part of it, and he loved me the way I loved him: wholly and completely, with every cell of my body and piece of my soul.

It mattered, how he loved me. It mattered a whole hell of a lot.

But it didn't change what I had to do next.

Chapter 35

Eli

The first thing I noticed when I pulled into my driveway was that Emma was sitting on my front stoop, her back resting against the door, her elbows wrapped around her knees.

Of course she was.

Because I had been looking for her all day, starting with her house. When she wasn't there, I had checked Town Hall. Then Hot and Wired, Sweet Things, Suzie's house, the food truck, Kate's house, and Goat's Tavern. I had checked every damn spot in Hart's Ridge except my own house. So yeah. I should have known, because there was literally nowhere else she could be.

I approached slowly. My futile search had left me hungry and grouchy, and there was a very real danger I was going to throw Emma over my shoulder and carry her into the house caveman-style.

She scrambled to her feet. "Hey. There you are." She smiled brightly. "Want to get a coffee?"

Coffee? I stopped. What the hell was she talking about? Why would we get coffee? Why would we do anything except fall into bed and tear each other's clothes off?

"I guess it's a little late for coffee." She squinted at the sun, low in the western sky, and frowned. "We could go to Goat's. Hang out with Luke for a bit."

I stared at her.

"Or if you don't feel like going out, we can stay here. Watch a show and order pizza. Whatever."

"I..." I looked at the sky, at the trees, left and right, trying to make sense of it. "Coffee? Luke? Pizza? What are you...what's going on?"

She blinked innocently. "I'm trying to be your friend."

"Friend." I wasn't sure I liked the sound of that at all.

"Yes. Because you love me in some way or other, and I want you in my life any way I can get you. And I think...I think being friends would be pretty great, because *you're* pretty great. But I realize you weren't expecting me, so if today doesn't work for you, then how about tomorrow?"

"Tomorrow?" I echoed.

"Tomorrow," she said firmly.

My heart bounded like an exuberant puppy. *Tomorrow*. She said it like she meant it. Like a promise. Maybe my mom broke promises, but Emma never would. Even if she did, I would be okay. I knew I would be. I would live. What I couldn't live with was never giving it a chance.

It was worth the risk. *She* was worth the risk. Although, I had to admit, it was a very small risk.

"I love you," I said.

"That's good to know." A smile bloomed on her face, slowly at first and then all at once, like the sun peeking out from behind a cloud. "I love you, too."

I laughed with pure joy. Bounded up the steps, wrapped my arms around her waist, and lifted her off her feet, making her laugh, too. I kissed her lightly, not trusting myself to take it too deeply. Once I started I wasn't going to stop for a good long while, and there were things I had to say first.

"I haven't said those words to anyone in a very long time. Not since my mother. And I hadn't heard them either, because she was the last person who said those words to me. It was what she said, when she left. She loved me. I think…I think somehow those things got twisted together in my mind. Love and goodbye."

She held on tight, squeezing me closer in sympathy. Not saying anything, just listening.

"It wasn't that I wasn't loved. My dad loved me. He did. As much as he was capable of. He never said it, and he showed it in odd ways. Looking back, he took better care of me than of himself. That isn't saying much, I know, but it was love just the same."

"And we loved you." Her fingers trailed the back of my neck. "Luke, Suzie, and I. We loved you."

I smiled crookedly. "Yeah. But we didn't say that kind of thing out loud, back then. Maybe if we had, I would have realized love doesn't always mean goodbye."

"Or maybe it would have been worse. I still would have…I shouldn't have done that. I shouldn't have frozen you out of my life."

"I've been thinking about that. And you know, once we had to be around each other again, it didn't take very long for it to turn into this. I wonder what would have happened if I had tried to talk to you, maybe after a month or so when you were cooled down, instead of letting you push me away. Not like harassed you or anything, but what if I had tried just once? Maybe twice? I don't know. It should have been you to take the first step, but that doesn't mean it couldn't have been me. Maybe we would have gotten here a lot sooner, maybe not. I don't know, but I do know that if it ever comes to that again, I'm not waiting around eight years for you to come to your senses. You've got a day, maybe two, before I come for you."

She laughed. "Well, thank god for that. This relationship won't survive if we're both stubborn jackasses." She rested her forehead against my chest. "But, seriously, Eli, I'm so sorry."

"No. You already apologized. You talked to your dad, and I know how hard that must have been for you. You did the work. It's my turn. I want you to hear this, because I don't want you carrying more guilt around. We've had enough of that."

"Okay," she whispered. Her eyes searched my face questioningly.

"It was easy for me to say this was about you. That you were like my mother. You had left me once and would do it again. But the truth was, it was me. I was a coward. Because if you were my mom, that made me my dad, and that...I couldn't take that. I told you what it was like, back then, but I never let you come to my house, because I didn't want you to see it for yourself. My dad did not react well to my mother leaving. He became a high-functioning alcoholic, and by that I mean that he could get up and go to work, but after work, he immediately stopped functioning. He was drunk from five o'clock until a good ways into his shift the next day, I would say. He just sat there, the TV on but not watching it, drinking until he passed out. I didn't want to become that."

"You would never become that, Eli," she said vehemently. "Never."

"It took me a minute to realize that. The thing is…God, Emma, I love you so much. Losing you is the worst thing I can imagine, the very worst. Yesterday, thinking I already had, it was the most painful experience I'd ever known, and I wouldn't wish that on anyone. But I survived it. And I'd survive it again, if it came to that. I'm not my dad. I can live without you, but I really, *really* don't want to."

"You don't have to. You will *never* have to."

"One more thing," I said.

She looked at me. "Yes?"

"If you still need a deputy mayor, I'll do it."

Her eyes lit up and she shrieked. "You will? Oh my God. I've got so many ideas. Christmas. A big tree lighting ceremony. Do you think we can pull it off?"

"Together. We can do anything together." I gave her hair a playful tug. "Actually, I have every faith that you could do it on your own. But you don't have to."

"Good. I would much rather do it with you."

Christmas was six months away. Longer than I had ever stayed with a woman. But I could see it now, our future together, laid out for the rest of our lives. It wouldn't be perfect. But it would be beautiful.

She was moving me, I suddenly realized. Guiding me up the steps, back to the house. Slightly awkwardly, as she was walking backwards and our bodies were tangled up together. I grinned against her hair.

I had a good feeling about where we were heading, together.

Thank you for reading Eli and Emma's story!
Want more Hart's Ridge?
Stay tuned for Kate's story,
DON'T CALL ME SWEETHEART.

It's not fake dating. It's practice dating.
Kate Gonzales thought she was ready to move on. After all, it'd been ten years since her military husband's death, and even single moms have needs. So, having a one-night stand with a sexy stranger seemed like such a good idea. Until she broke down in tears during the act. Turns out moving on is way more complicated than she thought...

Romance has always been problematic for Max Darlington. Having trouble connecting seems to be an unfortunate side effect of his time in the foster care system. But if he could learn to hold on to a sweetheart like Kate—someone who so beautifully expresses her emotions—he might finally be able to demolish the walls around his heart...

Kate doesn't know how to let go. Max doesn't know how to hold on. Maybe they can teach each other in a two-month practice relationship...but only if they can avoid breaking one potentially devastating rule.

No falling in love...

Reviews help readers find books!
Spreading the word by telling friends is a great way to help an author.
Thank you for taking the time to leave a review!

Acknowledgements

It's a strange and wonderful thing to watch a story become a book, and I am eternally grateful for everyone who helped make this possible. My editor, Mackenzie Walton, and cover designer, Wildheart Graphics, were amazing to work with. Liana and Lisa, thank you for listening to me talk about this book in between screaming about the awfulness of 2020. (2020, fuck you! I do not thank you for anything!) Rosie, thanks for the cooking lessons. I solemnly swear never to serve cold tortillas again.

And, always and forever, a huge thank you to my readers. You inspire me to put my butt in the chair and type these words every day. Thank you, thank you, thank you.

About the Author

Elizabeth Bright is a *USA Today* bestselling author of romance with heart, humor, and heat. When she's not writing defiant heroines and the men who adore them, Elizabeth can be found hiking and rock climbing. She lives in Washington, D.C. with her two daughters, who are every bit as stubborn and wonderful as the characters she writes.

Elizabeth loves to hear from readers! Please sign up for her newsletter or visit her website at to stay up to date on her latest releases.

Also By Elizabeth Bright

The Wicked Secrets Series

Twice as Wicked

Lady Gone Wicked

Wicked with the Scoundrel

The Duke's Wicked Wife

Hart's Ridge

Make Me Love You

Don't Call Me Sweetheart

Trust Me

Christmas at Hart's Ridge

Be the first to hear about new releases and sales!
Sign up for Elizabeth Bright's newsletter here:
www.elizabethbrightauthor.com

Made in United States
Orlando, FL
24 February 2025

58861719R00215